SPELLWOOD ACADEMY

KATE AVERY ELLISON

For Julie

CHAPTER ONE

YOU MIGHT THINK my story should begin with the acceptance letter to Spellwood Academy. The letter that arrived with the text still smoking from being written in fire on pages smelling of ancient forests and dusty crypts, delivered by spiders through the slot in my door.

But no. Everything started the night I almost died.

~

I never saw what hit me.

The rain was coming down in sheets as I steered my bike through the near-darkness in my small town of Everlade, North Carolina. Getting caught in the rain was one downside of not being able to afford a car. I hadn't meant to head home so late—and certainly not in a veritable monsoon—but I'd been stuck at the library an extra hour trying to finish my final paper for lit class. Absorbed as I was in Jane Austen's world of social graces, balls, and witty banter, I hadn't even realized how dark the sky had become until lightning illuminated my page.

I knew my mom was waiting tables at her second job, and Grandmother Azalea didn't drive due to her bad leg. So, I stayed until the library closed, and then I climbed on my bike and rode into the darkness, barely able to see more than a few feet ahead of me through the gloom of the torrential downpour.

Thankfully, I'd been wearing my helmet and my reflective vest that my mom insisted I take with me every time I biked anywhere that wasn't our neighborhood streets.

All I could remember was the shriek of screeching tires against wet pavement, and the sickening bounce of headlights spinning across the trees to the right of me, and the gut-wrenching shock of something slamming into me full force. It was like all my senses went white at the same time. Numb. I remember feeling soft, almost peaceful. The way it feels when you let out the breath you're holding and turn on your side before falling asleep.

And I was drifting like a piece of seaweed on the edge of a wave. Something—someone? —whispered sweetly in my ear, telling me to come home, telling me to let go. My soul unclenched and slipped through my ribs like smoke through bars.

Then—

Shouting. Blinding flashes of light in red and white.

I snapped back into my body with a jolt and felt hands touching me, then canvas against my back, and a dizzying sensation of being lifted. Rain wet my face. I was aware of pain, but faintly, like it was somewhere below me, threatening but not fully overtaking me.

Not yet.

Someone said something to me, a question, but I didn't understand them. The words ran together like rainwater, and I couldn't seem to turn my neck or remember how to open my mouth.

6

A hand squeezed mine. I squinted, trying to open my eyes, and fell back into an abyss of pain and then, mercifully, unconsciousness.

This time, my soul stayed where it was. The voice calling me from my body was gone.

~

I woke up in an ambulance, and I couldn't breathe. My eyes opened this time, just a crack that let in a blurry image of bouncing walls and double doors with windows to a dark, rain-soaked world. A paramedic leaned over me, but he was speaking to someone else. I heard him say, his voice oddly calm, "We're losing her." I smelled the sharp scents of medicine, rubber, and rubbing alcohol. I couldn't feel a thing. My body was numb, my legs two lumps covered by a blanket.

"Stay with me," the paramedic murmured as he put an oxygen mask over my nose and mouth.

My eyes closed again. I was already fading again. The abyss reached for me with shadowy arms, and I couldn't escape it.

I opened my eyes again inside a hospital. Harsh white lights spun above me. I lay face-up on a stretcher, and nurses were running with me down an impossibly long hallway. Shouts echoed around me, and I was still struggling to breathe despite the mask over my face.

The pain was like a blanket smothering me. I was in agony from my shoulders to my feet, and I couldn't even scream. I was frozen.

My tangled gazes with a doctor standing in a doorway as we rushed down the hall. He looked young and old at the same time. His hair was dark; his eyes were blue.

That was all I remembered before I faded again.

~

The next time I woke, I wasn't wearing the oxygen mask anymore. I stared up and saw round, saucer-like lights.

I shivered violently as the beeps and whispering sounds of medical machines filled the air. An operating room.

But I was alone in it. Alone and frightened.

No—there was a doctor, the same one with the blue eyes. He stood beside a sink at the wall, his back to me, but somehow, I still knew it was him. He had his hands braced against the counter and his head down. I saw his lips move as though he were reciting some silent mantra to himself.

"Doctor?" I croaked.

He turned. His eyes burned into mine with an intensity that stilled me.

"Am I dying?" I couldn't stop the tears that slipped from the corners of my eyes and slid down my cheeks to pool against my collarbone.

The young doctor approached me. He stopped beside me and smiled. It was a lean, quick flash of teeth. A gambler's smile. He reached down and placed a hand on my shoulder. His fingers were warm against my skin.

"You're going to live," he assured me, and then I blacked out again.

CHAPTER TWO

I WOKE UP in a regular hospital bed.

My mom was curled in a chair beside my pillow, asleep, her curly hair wrapped in a scarf, her face bare of makeup like she'd cried it all off. When I moved my arm, the IV in my hand tugged against my skin. The terrible, crushing pain was gone, replaced by a whimper of discomfort in comparison. I breathed in, testing my lungs, and they filled with air.

I turned my head and whispered, "Mom."

She woke immediately and leaped to her feet. Her hands fluttered over me, anxious and unlike her. "Baby," she gasped, her eyes filling with tears. "How are you feeling? Are you in pain?"

"Thirsty," I croaked.

She lunged across the room for a pitcher of water and a glass that sat on a rolling table at the other end of the bed. "Water?" she asked, turning to me with the pitcher clutched in her hand like it was the solution to world peace. "Or juice? I can get you apple juice from the nurse's station. They also have tea. No coffee for you yet, of course, but—"

"Let's start with water," I said, smiling at her. My eyes were leaking a little. I could tell she'd been frantic. I was sorry about that. I hated to think of her in pain, thinking I might die.

My mom poured me water, splashing a little in her excitement, and brought the cup to me. I gingerly tried to sit up, and she pressed the button to raise the top part of the bed.

9

"Here," she said, helping me lift the edge of the cup to my mouth.

As I drank, she kissed the top of my head repeatedly. "Thought I'd lost you," she muttered into my hair. "I've never been so scared in my life. Oh, my poor baby."

"Mom," I whispered. I didn't want her to worry about that. My mom had a tendency to worry endlessly if she didn't stop herself, even after something was over.

Her eyes widened. "Let me text Grandmother Azalea. She's waiting to hear how you are."

As she fumbled with her phone, I finished the water and set the glass down on the bedside table. Questions churned in my head. I remembered flashes from before—the ambulance, the operating room. I had no idea what time it was, or how long I'd been asleep. The shades were closed on the window, but I could see faint light that looked like dawn.

"Did you get here while I was in the operating room?" I asked Mom.

She lifted her head. Her brow wrinkled. "Operating room?"

"For my chest?" I said, just as confused. Hadn't they told her? "The doctor was a young guy, dark hair?"

She shook her head. "Your doctor is a woman, Kyra."

A knock came at the door. The doctor. She stepped inside and smiled at me. She was my mother's age, perhaps, with yellow hair and crow's feet at the edges of her eyes, which were brown.

"How are you feeling?" she asked. Her voice was brisk but kind.

"A lot better," I said. "I was in so much pain before, but my chest and stomach aren't hurting at all now."

"Your chest and stomach?" She wrote this down as if it were something of interest.

"Y-yes," I said. "Where all the blood was."

She looked at me strangely.

"My mom and I were discussing earlier—I was in an operating room, but my mom seems to think—" I paused. "Where is the doctor who helped me? The one in the operating room? He had blue eyes. I wanted to thank him."

The doctor came and sat down on the edge of my bed. She pulled a small flashlight from her pocket and checked my eyes. The place between her eyebrows pinched. "Can you tell me what month and day it is?"

"Er, well, how long have I been in here?" I hedged as I grappled mentally to understand.

If they were asking me questions like this, then they thought I had a head injury.

I didn't understand.

What about the doctor? I hadn't hallucinated that.

Had I?

The doctor's brows drew together at my answer. I amended it.

"It's almost May," I said. "School's almost out. I'm a senior... I'm graduating..."

"How many fingers am I holding up?" She held up three.

I sighed and answered the rest of her questions. When she'd finished, I said, "Can somebody tell me what's going on?"

"You were knocked off your bike by a car," my mom said. "You sprained your wrist, bruised your hip, and got a nasty bump on your head. The painkillers they gave you made you sleep a lot."

Her eyes were watchful. As if she knew something I didn't. Or maybe I was imagining things.

It had been a long night.

I looked down at my left arm, which was covered in a bandage. "Oh."

"Sometimes patients have vivid dreams," the doctor offered with a smile.

It wasn't a dream. The denial rose to my lips, but I didn't say the words. I forced myself to nod as if I agreed with her.

After she left, my mom hugged me again.

"Mom," I whispered. "It felt really real."

She smoothed my hair and pressed her forehead against mine. "You're safe now. Let's focus on that."

I went home a few hours later.

My letter to the academy arrived thirteen days later.

CHAPTER THREE

MY MOM AND I lived with my grandmother, Azalea Brown. We'd always lived with her, because my mom was a single mother, and my father was nowhere to be found. I'd never even met him. We didn't need him—we were the perfect three all by ourselves. I grew up calling us the Three Musketeers. My Grandmother Azalea, on the other hand, liked to refer wryly to the three of us the Three Blind Mice.

But we were happy.

We lived in a tiny house plunked down in the middle of a terrible neighborhood. Our yard was an oasis of sunflowers and sculptures amid the yards of tangled weeds and broken-down cars. The shutters were blue, and my grandmother's sculptures and clay pots cluttered the front step and lined our walkway. When I was a little girl, I'd sometimes pretended our front yard was the domain of a wicked witch who'd turned everyone and everything to stone.

Somehow, we'd always escaped break-ins. I used to tell myself as a child that it was the power of the wicked witch that protected us.

~

The letter arrived on a warm, muggy morning.

I was eating breakfast when I heard the clatter of the mail flap. My mom shouted for me to get the mail, and I rose absently to retrieve the delivered papers.

I froze in the hall at the sight of the spiders. For a moment, my mind refused to process what I was seeing as a gray mass dripped through the flap, crawling down the door and into a heaving, rippling puddle on our mat.

I heard Grandmother Azalea call my name, but I was rooted to the floor as I watched the knot of spiders convulse around something. An envelope.

Nothing about this made sense.

As my grandmother's footsteps rattled the floorboards, the spiders streaked back for the door, leaving the envelope behind.

"Kyra?" my grandmother asked from the other room, and there was a note of something in her voice, something like alarm, as if she sensed a change in the air.

Grandmother Azalea was a tall, lean woman, with golden-brown eyes that could scorch you or warm you to your bones depending on her mood. Her hair was black and curly, threaded with silver, but her smooth, dark brown skin had no wrinkles, and she was fit as a yoga instructor besides a withered left leg. I'd often wondered if she'd ever had injections to maintain that perfect skin, but I never dared to ask. She was a sculptor now, wresting beauty from clay in the shed behind our tiny house, and she'd just come inside. She still wore her clay-splattered apron, and she had a smear of mud on her left cheek.

"Kyra—" she began, but then she saw the envelope lying on the mat, and the last few of the spiders disappearing through the flap, and she let out a sound that was something between a gasp and a moan, as if she'd seen a corpse. She staggered, her hand flying to the wall to brace herself, and I shouted for my mom as I grabbed her arm to steady her.

My mom came running. She was in her work uniform, her makeup half-finished. She looked at my grandmother in alarm.

"The spiders are gone," I told Grandmother Azalea. My head was ringing, because whatever had happened with the spiders was definitely not normal, but I was focused on my grandmother. She had turned a shade of gray that made me wonder if we were going to have to call an ambulance.

"Spiders?" my mom demanded. She looked around the floor at her feet nervously. "What's going on?"

Then her gaze fell on the letter, and something in her face changed. She pulled back her shoulders and closed her lips into a line.

Whatever the letter was, my mom knew what it was.

Grandmother Azalea sank onto the couch. She was still staring at the envelope. "It's not the spiders, Kyra," she panted. "I... I can't believe they've found... I thought..."

I looked at the envelope. "Who?"

Something about my grandmother's tone sent shivers like spiders down my spine. The way she'd said *they*, as if talking about some ancient evil. As if grasping zombie arms were able to smash through our windows and grope for us.

"Pick it up," Grandmother Azalea said in resignation, nodding at the envelope.

I hesitated. I trusted my grandmother implicitly, but there had been a lot of spiders.

"The arachnids are gone," she murmured. "They were never real, anyway. Just an illusion. A joke..."

15

I didn't understand. I crossed the room and retrieved the envelope. The paper was warm.

"Open it," Grandmother Azalea commanded, and she sounded as if she were ordering me to dip my hand in acid. Regret, fear, and concern mingled in her voice. And one final emotion.

Fury.

The envelope was sealed with a heavy dollop of black wax, stamped with a symbol I didn't know. I gentled broke the seal and drew back the flap.

Inside was a folded piece of paper and a bundle of what looked like powdered herbs. No, parchment. Heavy, with ragged edges. I drew it out and unfolded it.

The letters on the page smoked as if they had been burned into the parchment only seconds ago. They were the color of charcoal.

At the top was my name. Kyra Solschild.

A fizzle of shock broke over me. I shot a glance at Grandmother Azalea, who nodded grimly at me.

"Keep reading," she said. "Aloud, please."

I did as she asked. "Kyra Solschild, born of fae blood, we are pleased to extend an invitation to the year one class at Spellwood Academy. Please bring this letter, a vial of your tears, and a captured laugh to the address listed below a month and a fortnight before Summertide's Eve. Be advised that you will also be required to submit a drop of blood and a lock of hair—"

I broke off, looking up at my mom and grandmother. This was nonsense. No, madness. Born of fae blood? A vial of tears? A captured laugh? A nervous giggle escaped me. "What kind of sick joke is this?"

But neither my mom nor my grandmother laughed at the absurdity.

Instead, they looked grim.

"How did that letter find us? I thought we were well hidden," Grandmother Azalea said angrily. "I've spent a fortune in charms. I've been paying that fool spellcaster for years—"

"It was me," my mom interrupted. "I did it. I told Spellwood where she was. I wrote to them last week—"

"If you told Spellwood, then they will know, if they don't know already!" Grandmother Azalea burst out.

"What's Spellwood?" I cried. "What's going on?" I looked between them, but they were focused on each other. My words failed to penetrate their bubble of fury.

My grandmother fell silent as my mom clasped and unclasped her hands nervously.

"Grandmother Azalea?" I tried again, feeling like a child.

"I told the school directly," my mom insisted then. "*They* don't know."

"Who is *they*?" I asked.

Grandmother Azalea's eyes scorched as bright as midday suns. "Why?" she spat finally. "Whatever possessed you to—"

"It was the accident," my mom burst out. "Someone is obviously trying to kill her. And then someone else used magic to save her. Something is going on, Mom, and we have to take action."

"Someone is trying to kill me?" My mind flashed back to the rain-soaked night. The ambulance. The pain. The confusion. My mom's murmured assurances that it was all fine, that I was fine. The

17

look on her face that seemed to contradict her words.

And that doctor, the one with the blue eyes, the one everybody insisted was a hallucination or a dream...

I turned my arm over and looked at my sprained wrist. An inkling of a suspicion filled my head, and I began to unwind the bandages. My mom had been doing it, checking to make sure everything was well, telling me not to look because "it might make you feel queasy, sweetie." Giving me things to keep me busy while she examined my injury, like a funny video someone sent her, or a catalogue full of clothing she was never going to buy. She'd kept me distracted. I hadn't ever seen the injury.

The bandage fell away. I looked at my arm, and my stomach clenched.

A mark lay on my wrist. A dark purple-black bruise, streaked like ink beneath my skin. I drew in a sharp breath, my stomach twisting. Something about the shape of it seemed wrong. Intentional, almost.

"She isn't going," my grandmother was saying, her voice crackling with anger. "She belongs with us, not with that world."

"She has to go!" my mom snapped back. "If she doesn't—"

"It was never sprained, was it?" I asked, my voice sharp as a steak knife.

They both fell silent. My mom winced as she picked up the fallen bandage and folded it over and over into a square in her lap. She bit her lip. "No. But I wanted to protect you as long as I could. Until I was sure."

"Sure of what?" I demanded.

18

"Sure you were in danger."

"And the doctor?" I asked. "He wasn't a dream. I was really hurt, and he... and he..." I fell short of saying the thought in my head.

"Someone healed you. I don't know who." My mom was pale.

"And now, you want to send me away to some place called... Spellwood?" My throat thickened with tears. I stared at her.

"You did this," Grandmother Azalea said to my mom in a voice low and laced with fury. "You were always determined to exile her to Spellwood not matter what I said."

"I saved her," my mom shot back. "Look at her arm, Azalea. That's a death mark on her. Someone tried to kill her. She has to go. She'll be safe there."

She only ever called my grandmother by her first name when they were fighting.

"I—what?" I cried out, looking between their faces. "Mom, what's going on? Who are you talking about? What's a death mark?"

"You're frightening her," Grandmother Azalea accused. "Look at your daughter. Look what you've done. My charms would have been enough."

"You're both frightening me," I snapped. "And the creepy letter delivered by spiders that talks about giving someone a vial of my tears isn't helping. Stop fighting and tell me what's going on. I'm not going anywhere unless I agree, and I can't agree to something I don't understand. So, tell me!"

My mom put both hands over her eyes and sighed deeply. She wiped at tears and locked eyes with Grandmother Azalea.

"It's time," my mom said.

CHAPTER FOUR

WE SAT AROUND the kitchen table with steaming mugs of Grandmother Azalea's herbal tea in front of us. The smell of the tea filled the room with hints of lavender, chamomile, and honey, but nobody drank. The letter lay in the middle of the table. My grandmother's long fingers tapped against the mug that she wasn't drinking from. The light from the garden streamed through the window in a golden haze, and I could hear birds chirping in the bushes. But inside, the atmosphere was grim.

"Tell me," I demanded when I could stand the suffocating silence no longer. "Tell me what's going on."

My grandmother started to speak, but my mom put a hand out to silence her.

"Please, let me," Mom said. "It's my story to tell, really."

"It's both our stories," Grandmother Azalea countered, but Mom persisted.

"Please."

My grandmother jerked her head in a nod.

My mom took a deep breath. "Kyra, your... your father wasn't, ah, wasn't exactly human."

Alarm pierced me. "What?" I managed to squeak out.

Wasn't human.

Born of fae blood...

I tried the word on my tongue. "Fae."

Saying it sent a shiver of confusion through my limbs. Fae. An old word from the periphery of my memories—bedtime stories from my Grandmother

Azalea rose in my mind, how she'd read fairy tales to me at nighttime and scoff at the depictions of the tiny, dainty fairies as if offended.

"That isn't how the fae are," she'd sometimes murmur when she thought I was too young to remember, too sleepy to hear her. Part of me thought her eccentric, part of me thought her charmingly old fashioned. Believing in fairies.

"Yes," my mom said. "He was one of the fae."

Grandmother Azalea's oddness was one thing. But here was my mom, my sensible, hard-working, no-nonsense-but-still-a-little-bit-overly-emotional mother looking me in the eye and telling me that fairies were real. The same woman who told me flatly that getting pregnant from a hot tub was an urban legend.

"My father was a fairy?" I said. The words sounded utterly ridiculous in the stillness of the kitchen.

"He was fae," my grandmother said. "Not quite the same thing. Calling one of the fae folk a fairy is the utmost of insults." She sighed. "I'm afraid we have woefully neglected your education. It was done in the name of safety... I had hoped... well, never mind now. What's done is done."

"I was young," my mom explained. "I thought I might be able to live with him in—in their world."

Their world.

My head was spinning. I had a million questions, but I let her speak.

"I thought we were in love," my mom continued. Her face was pale, and her cheeks flushed at the memory. "He made me promises. Declarations. He talked about marriage. And when I became unexpectedly pregnant, I thought he would be happy. But instead, he vanished. He left me."

I thought about my last name. I spoke it aloud, a question. "Kyra... Solschild. Sol's child? Like the sun?"

My mom shook her head. "I made up the name for your birth certificate. It was a tiny piece of connection to him, a joke between us. You see, he was... he was from the summer court, and he was like the sun in my sky, and I met him at Summertide, on the solstice..."

Summer court. Summertide. More words I didn't understand.

"I called him Sol," my mom said. "And he called me Luna."

She lifted her mug and took a gulp. When she lowered it, she said, "The family sent his older brother to find me in the mortal world and demand I give them the baby, or else they'd kill me. I told them I'd had a miscarriage." Her gaze was remote. "I think he wanted to believe me, because he put down his sword and went away without questioning my story."

"His sword?" I repeated faintly.

"Yes," she said, and took another sip from her mug. "He had a silver sword that glowed with an inner blue fire. He wore it on his back in a golden sheath. He drew it in the living room and stood over me like an archangel of death. But I don't think he wanted to kill you. I think that's why he believed me." She shook her head and shuddered.

I shuddered too.

"So, we hid you," Grandmother Azalea said. "We cast the charms and paid for the spells, and hid you from them. We moved a few times. But now..."

"What?" I said. "Now they're going to come for me with a sword again? Try to chop off my head?"

"No," my mom said. "You are grown now. You are not a tiny baby so easily taken and disposed of. But they will learn of your existence in time, and they will not be pleased with me."

"Am I in danger still, though?" I asked. My throat felt tight. My skin prickled all over. Half of me still reeled from the revelation—fairies were real. Magic was real. Either that, or both my grandmother and my mom were insane. But I'd seen the letter delivered by spiders. I'd have to be insane too. I looked at the mark on my wrist. "Was it my father's family that did this?"

"No," my mom said. "Your father was from the summer court. This was the work of one of the darker, unseelie courts. The water, winter, and dark courts—their magic has this dark signature."

"How can you be sure?" I asked.

"Look at it," my grandmother said. "It is like ink. It is their putrid work, I'm sure of it."

I stared down at it again. The dark tendrils almost seemed to shimmer, as if a handful of night sky had slipped into my veins and seeped stardust into the bruises. I rubbed my fingers across the mark, frightened. What was this... this stuff under my skin?

"Magic," my mom said.

"Why do they want me dead?" My throat constricted at the words.

My mom shook her head. "I don't know. It could have something to do with my past."

I swallowed hard. "Will they try again? Whoever did this?"

"You will be protected at Spellwood," my mom said firmly. "That is why I enrolled you."

Grandmother Azalea let out a huff, but my mom cut off whatever she'd been about to say. "Their spells and protections are some of the finest among the fae. She will learn how to protect herself there."

"Tell me about Spellwood," I whispered. The name alone conjured visions of somewhere mysterious and dark, a manor built of forests, the floors strewn with fairy dust.

"Spellwood is a school for those born with a mixture of mortal and fae blood," my mom said.

Born of fae blood, the letter had said.

"There, you will learn about your heritage—your fae heritage—and about what it takes to live in that world. You will make friends, alliances. It'll be temporary—just until we can figure out who's trying to hurt you, and what's going on. Just as long as you need to be safe."

"Then," my grandmother hastened to add, "you can come home."

"But I know nothing about that world," I protested. "Surely everyone else will have been there for years, and be close to graduating—"

"The school is those of your age," she said. "More of a college than anything else, although some start younger. You will not be the only one beginning their first year. Most of mixed blood begin attendance between their sixteenth and eighteenth year. You will be eighteen in three months. You are the perfect age to go."

I looked down at my mug of tea, which had gone cold. "When do I leave? The letter said—n" I picked it up to reread the line. "—a month and a fortnight

24

before Summertide's Eve. What is Summertide's Eve?"

"One of the fae holidays. The solstice." My mom was looking at the calendar that hung on the fridge, then counted on her fingers. "She would need to leave... tomorrow."

The word fell like a stone. My grandmother's lips whitened.

"Tomorrow!" I burst out, aghast. "But I haven't even made up my mind yet."

"The letter was late," Grandmother Azalea muttered.

"Or someone didn't want her to receive it," my mom said.

They exchanged a glance and then looked at me.

"Well?" Grandmother Azalea asked.

The weight of my decision pressed on my shoulders, but at the same time, it seemed clear. My indomitable grandmother was pale as bone. My mom had gone behind her mother's back to secure this invitation. I trusted them both.

"I'll go," I said.

My mom sighed. She pressed a hand to her eyes, then looked pointedly at my grandmother. "We will not waste time while you are gone. We'll find out what's going on, Kyra. I promise you."

I swallowed the lump in my throat and nodded. I was scared.

After a moment, Grandmother Azalea rose and went to the cupboard. She took out two glass jars, one as slender as a finger, the other wide at the base and narrow at the top. She handed the bigger one to me first.

"We have to capture a laugh," she said.

I stared down into the jar. "How? Do I just... laugh into it?"

They nodded.

I cleared my throat. I summoned a chuckle. It was forced, nervous. It skittered into the jar with an echo, and then Grandmother Azalea pressed a cork into the opening and set the jar aside. She handed me the vial.

"Tears next," she said briskly.

I wasn't sure how to make myself cry on command. "Do they have to be real tears? Can I poke myself in the eye?"

My mom and Grandmother Azalea frowned at each other thoughtfully.

We ended up watching videos online featuring reunions between lost puppies and their owners, something that never failed to move me. The video, coupled with the dizzying revelations of the day, made the tears come easily. I sniffled, my eyes pooling with a few salty tears when a white-whiskered Labrador was reunited with his elderly owner after weeks apart, and my mom pressed the vial into my hand. I held the vial to my cheek and captured seven tears as they fell, and they clustered in a thick liquid at the bottom of the glass.

"You got enough," Grandmother Azalea said, and took it from my hand.

They packed the vials, along with the letter of acceptance, in a leather satchel Grandmother Azalea produced from deep within one of her closets.

"What about clothes?" I asked as we stood in my grandmother's bedroom. I held the satchel. The room smelled like baby powder and sage. The curtains were drawn over the windows, blocking the cheerful sunlight outside. It was noon. My stomach gurgled, but I had no appetite.

"They'll have uniforms there," my mom explained.

"Is there a website or brochure I could look at?" I asked.

Both my mom and Grandmother Azalea turned to stare at me.

"This is a secret school run by fae," my mom said. "There are no websites, Kyra."

I nodded, crestfallen. I was terrified. Having some pictures, testimonials, anything of that kind would set my mind a little bit at ease. "Did you go to the school?"

"I did not," my mom said. "I..." She paused. Looked at my grandmother carefully. "Although I could have, I suppose."

Wait a moment. "Does that mean you...?"

My mom's face tightened slightly. "Yes, I am part fae as well. One quarter."

"Grandmother Azalea," I said, turning to the older woman. "More secrets?"

She sighed. "It is a long story, one I do not have the energy to tell you now. He was a commoner among the fae, a half-mortal himself. We were married. We lived in their world for a time. When he died, I came here. Raised your mother alone. She was not aware of her heritage when she met your father."

I looked at them, and heaviness lodged in my chest like a brick. Two single mothers. Two women who'd carried heavy secrets for most of their lives. They'd kept all of this from me. They'd told me lies my entire life. Part of me wanted to scream at them. I was shaking.

I sank down on Grandmother Azalea's bed and put my head in my hands.

I was part fairy. Fae. Whatever. My uncle had tried to kill me. My grandmother had lived in another world. There was a mark on my arm from a fae assassin.

"What else have you not told me?" I asked. I felt oddly calm now. As if I were drugged.

"There is much to know," Grandmother Azalea whispered. She brushed a hand across my cheek. "But you need to sleep. You need rest."

The tea. Had the tea been drugged?

"It was only my calming herbs," my grandmother said, smoothing her hand across my hair.

"Wait," I said. "The doctor. The one with the blue eyes. Who—?"

"A fae, probably. Enchanted everyone to forget what he did."

"But who was he?"

"I don't know," my mom admitted, and her mouth tightened. She didn't seem pleased about it. "But whoever he is, he saved your life. Sometimes rogue fae roam the mortal world, doing good deeds if it pleases them."

My eyelids felt heavy. I tried to remember the face of the doctor, but all I could think of were his vivid eyes and his long, clever fingers.

"Sleep," my mom urged me. "You've had a great shock. You need time to process. When you wake, we will talk more and pack the rest of your things. Right now, your grandmother and I need to take care of a few things. Sleep, love."

So, I slept.

CHAPTER FIVE

I WOKE LATER that evening from a nap that felt like an age. My mouth tasted stale, and my stomach cramped with hunger, but my thoughts were clear. When I reviewed the facts—I was part fae, someone had tried to kill me, I was being shipped off to a school for half-fairies tomorrow—I did not feel the same clawing panic as before. I still felt fear, but it was tempered by curiosity now.

What kind of place would Spellwood be?

The name conjured images of thick forests and dark passages and towers covered in vines. Claws and teeth and dark horses. I shivered.

I went downstairs and found my mom and Grandmother Azalea at the table with a clutter of bizarre items spread before them on a leather cloth. Bottles, vials, quills, stones, and other arcane and otherworldly trinkets.

"What are these?" I asked. I touched a finger to a tiny dagger the size of my hand. A purple gemstone glittered at its hilt.

"These are for you to take to Spellwood if you wish," my mom said. "We went through our old things while you napped. Some of these might prove useful to you." She pointed to different jars, naming some of the herbs and crystals they contained. Things I'd never heard of before. "Here we have pink quartz. Blue asterine. In this, feathercorn. There, fishwinkle dust."

I brushed my fingers over the things, wondering.

"What calls to you?" Grandmother Azalea asked. "Choose anything that seems like it ought to be yours."

In the end, I selected the dagger, a necklace with a jeweled leaf dangling at the end, and a bottle filled with purple shards of crystal. The necklace was my grandmother's, she said, and the knife and bottle of crystals were my mother's.

After that, we made dinner together. The three of us, like we always did, except this time my chest was heavy with the knowledge that tomorrow I was going somewhere unknown. Spellwood. The sound of it tasted thorny on my tongue. I silently chanted it to myself as we boiled the noodles, chopped the tomatoes and fresh basil from Grandmother Azalea's garden, and seasoned the sauce.

As we ate, I asked more questions.

"What happens if I go to this school? Will that make me a high school dropout? Will I be unable to graduate?"

My mom toyed with her food. "I've already spoken with your teachers. You've finished most of your final projects, and you've got all A's, so you can be exempt from your exams. We'll tell them you have a traumatic brain injury from the accident, have to see a specialist out of state and receive treatment, and cannot finish the last few weeks. They'll still give you your diploma."

"And if they need any persuading, we can buy a spell for it," Grandmother Azalea added.

"And my friends at school? What will I tell them?" I protested, although honestly, I knew they'd all easily accept the story of my brain injury. I wasn't particularly close with anyone this year. I'd had a childhood best friend named Lulu, but I hadn't spoken to her in years, and my last best friend, Amanda Deere, had moved away two years ago. Since then, I'd drifted between friend groups without putting down any real roots.

"What was my father's name?" I couldn't believe I hadn't asked that yet. Somehow, it had slipped my mind entirely. "You always told me it was John."

My mom looked down at her spaghetti. "That was a lie. I'm sorry, Kyra. Your father's name was Gajonadral. I referred to him as John when we were in the mortal world."

"And... his last name? Do the fae have last names?"

"I do not know his family name," she admitted. "Only that he came from the summer court."

Gajonadral. I memorized the unfamiliar syllables. A hunger to know more about him gnawed at me even as I loathed him for abandoning my mom and me, and worse, sending his brother to destroy me afterward.

When we'd finished eating, we cleared the table and loaded the dishes. My grandmother made more lavender and chamomile tea. She handed me a cup. "With valerian root," she said, brushing a hand down my cheek. "For calmness."

My face must've betrayed my anxiety.

We sat in the living room, our feet curled beneath us, and I asked her to tell me about her life among the fae. She was hesitant, her words like water in a broken cistern, slow-flowing and at times unclear. She described a conifer forest lit by distant lights that winked among the treetops in colors of pink, gold, and pale blue, of men with teeth like needles and horses with feathers that covered their hooves and sprouted from their manes and tails. She told me of palaces built beneath hills, and out of interlocking trees, and from crystal stones. It was all wonderful, heady, and strange, and her descriptions were like something out of a fever dream.

"He had horns on his head," Grandmother Azalea said. "Beautiful, curving horns, like a ram's." Her expression turned dreamy and remote, and I wondered how she could find such a thing beautiful, but I didn't say that. I stayed quiet and listened, afraid that if I spoke, I might break the spell she was under.

Finally, when the clock read midnight, my grandmother and mom told me to go to bed. And while I lay beneath the covers, my stomach twisting with uncertainty, I heard the soft squeak of feet against the floor, and then my mom slipped into my room, lay down beside me, and cuddled me until we both fell asleep in the darkness.

I slept fitfully, my sleep threaded with dreams of men with faces like rams and horses with teeth like needles. I woke abruptly to the sun in my eyes and my mom gone. In the kitchen, I heard the sound of a teapot whistling.

I rose and went into the bathroom to stare at my face in the mirror.

I looked human. My eyes were hazel, my skin dark olive and faintly freckled, my hair black and snarled with a hint of my Grandmother Azalea's curls. I had no needle teeth, no horns. No fairy wings.

Was this really what I wanted? To disappear to this strange school I'd never heard of before?

I grabbed my toothbrush and brushed my teeth while I thought about it. No, I didn't want to go. I didn't want to leave my home, my mom, or

Grandmother Azalea. I didn't want to leave my life and my friends. I didn't have a lot of plans beyond graduation—I was going to go to the local community college, get a boring degree in something like business, and get a job to help pay the bills. But I wanted to stay here. We were the Three Musketeers. My grandmother, my mom, and me.

I didn't want to go.

Right?

Actually, if I was honest with myself, somewhere amid the pit of terrible anxiety in my stomach was a flicker of excitement. My grandmother's stories had taken root, and part of me wondered—what sort of things might be at this school? Would I see horses with feathers and lights among the trees? The words they'd used—Summertide and fishwinkle—drifted through my head.

A knock sounded at the door, and my mom peeked inside.

"We made your favorite breakfast," she said. "After we eat..." She paused, and I knew.

It was almost time.

~

Mom told me it didn't matter what I wore, but of course, it did. Even if I was going to change into a uniform later, first impressions were still first impressions.

But what exactly did one wear to a school for people with fae blood in their veins? Should I wear all black? Go all-out with contouring? Dust my cheekbones and eyelids with a glittery highlighter?

In the end, I kept things simple. My favorite pair of jeans, a hunter-green shirt that made my boobs

33

look fantastic and left my olive skin glowing, and makeup and mascara that accentuated my eyes.

I felt casually confident, which is what I wanted to project.

After breakfast—which had been more of a brunch, considering the fact that I hadn't woken until almost noon—my mom and Grandmother Azalea looked at the clock and then each other They pressed the leather satchel into my hands and walked with into my grandmother's room. Grandmother Azalea put a necklace around my neck—a locket with both their pictures in it.

"It's enchanted," she told me. "Leave a scrap of paper inside, and we'll be able to read it and respond. You can also send and receive proper letters at the school."

We stood before my grandmother's mirror, and she spoke a few words and blew the herbs from the letter onto the shiny surface, dusting it lightly.

"Are you performing magic?" I asked.

"It's a simple spell sent by the school," Grandmother Azalea replied. "Anyone can perform it with the right ingredients."

The mirror rippled and winked, and a cloudy image appeared within it as if we were looking through a screen.

I reached out a hand and touched the surface of the mirror, and it reminded me of water, with a brush of resistance to my fingers that gave under the slightest pressure. My fingers slipped through the mirror and into what felt like warm air on the other side before I yanked them back in astonishment.

I grabbed my mom's hands and squeezed as panic threatened to overwhelm me.

"Where does it lead?" I gasped.

"To a place between this world and the fae one," Grandmother Azalea said calmly. "It borders the fae lands. You will travel there with one step. It's completely painless."

"How will I get back to you?" I asked. "How will I contact you?"

"Use the necklace if you need to talk," my mom said. "And send us letters. We'll see you soon. Remember, we'll be working to fix this. We'll bring you home as soon as we can." She swiped at a tear that shimmered at the corner of her eye.

"We'll see you at Wintertide," Grandmother Azalea added.

"When is that?" I exclaimed.

"Six months," she promised, and then the mirror rippled again.

I took a deep, steadying breath, kissed them both on the cheek, and stepped through the glass.

CHAPTER SIX

I STEPPED THROUGH the mirror and onto soft green grass, caught a glimpse of lawn and a stone manor beyond, and then I promptly collided with someone else who had also just winked into existence. The force of the blow knocked me backward onto the springy lawn. The locket around my neck thumped against my collarbone.

"I beg your pardon!" the other person, a girl, said in a startled tone. "Are you all right?"

The girl bent over me in concern. She had warm brown skin, straight black hair, and eyes that were slitted like cat's eyes. She reached down to help me up, and I saw that her hands each had six fingers. But they felt human and solid when she clasped mine, and she smiled at me with a friendly look.

"I'm fine," I gasped. I had just noticed that she had the faintest striped markings along her temples and arms, and I was still processing this, trying not to stare. "And you?"

"Not a scratch," she assured me.

We were standing, I noticed, in front of a lichen-flecked stone archway. It looked like a doorway, but the other side was just more lawn.

It must be the doorway that we'd both stepped through to enter Spellwood. We must have both chosen the same moment to enter. Hence our collision, I supposed.

I allowed myself to look around, taking in the scenery.

So, this was Spellwood Academy.

A jewel-green lawn stretched in either direction, surrounded by stone buildings that rose toward a cloudless blue sky. The air was warm and smelled faintly sweet, like roses. Turrets and parapets towered overhead. I saw a domed roof capping a rounded stone tower that was covered in red-tipped, thorny vines. A statue of a winged horse perched on the top, rearing on two legs with one hoof pointed toward the sky.

It was breathtakingly beautiful, and something in my chest lurched with the feeling that I was somewhere that might be called home, and even though the place was unfamiliar, it had an air to it that made me feel that I belonged there. Not in the cozy way that a child belongs in the arms of her mother, but the way a horse belongs on a windswept plain. It was, I suppose, in my blood.

"My name is Tearly," the girl said, cutting into my thoughts and pulling my attention back to her. "I'm a third year. Have we met before? I've never seen you before, so you must be new."

"This is my first year," I said. "My name is Kyra—"

Before I could finish, the archway flashed with a bright light, and someone else ran into us as they exited the stone archway. Another girl, this one tall and willowy, with skin as pale as milk and eyes that were completely black. She tossed her pale, flowing hair and bared her teeth at us. They were pointed at the ends. "Get out of the way, mortals," she hissed.

"We're all part mortal here," Tearly said, but the pale girl only flashed a smile bright with promises of pain and blood.

"I might have a few splashes of human blood," she said in a voice as cold and sweet frozen sap.

"But I will live for a thousand years, and you'll be dead at eighty-five."

"I should think living a thousand years would get monotonous after a while," Tearly responded fearlessly. "Think of all those trips to the dentist."

"You might be a renowned archer, Tearly," the girl said, "but you're not invincible. Think of what happened to your family."

Tearly's face tightened. "Better move along, or you won't live to see those thousand years."

The pale girl only sniffed and then stalked away, toward a stone mansion at the far end of the lawn.

I let out a shuddering breath. I felt as if a cold winter wind had whipped through my clothes and chilled me to the bone.

Tearly's expression shifted, and she tucked away her scowl like it was a tattered handkerchief she didn't want anyone to see. She turned back to me with a smile in place.

I wondered what the cold girl with the black eyes had meant about her family, but I wasn't about to ask. The words had clearly been intended to hurt Tearly.

"Better take a step back," Tearly said with a short laugh under her breath, and she grabbed my elbow and steered me a few steps away. "Don't want any more collisions with the more unfriendly of the folk. Come on. I'll walk you to the registration desk. We're early, so if you get your room assignment now, you can claim the best bed."

"Who was that?" I asked, glancing in the direction the pale, terrifying girl had gone. I heartily hoped she wasn't my roommate.

"Her name is Isadora," Tearly said. "A fourth-year student. She's from the winter court. The puns practically write themselves, don't they?"

"Is it true?" I asked.

"What, that I'm a renowned archer? I don't like to brag, but I am the best shot at Spellwood Academy." Tearly grinned at me and flipped her hair away from her eyes. "I know that wasn't what you were asking. Is what true?"

I swallowed hard. Just asking gave me chills. "Will she live a thousand years?"

"Probably," Tearly said with a shrug. "She's the daughter of a queen. She has a lot of magic in her veins—and up her butt, judging by her attitude."

I was startled into laughter.

"But don't let me fool you," Tearly added, hooking an arm through mine and pulling me along as she started to walk toward the largest of the stone buildings. "She's dangerous and mean. You should probably steer clear of her. I'm just a glutton for punishment, as my father would say. I provoke everyone. But don't be like me. Don't shoot witty comebacks at the scary-looking students. Especially the fourth years. They aren't afraid of anyone."

"Okay," I said. "Any other advice?"

Tearly tapped a finger against her chin thoughtfully. "Don't go into the crypt at night or the labyrinth at all. Don't attend any Basilisk parties—they're dangerous. And don't attend any Toadcurdle parties—they're boring. Don't ever go hiking in the south woods alone at night. Don't go into the west woods alone either, come to think of it. Don't eat the meat in the cafeteria on Tuesdays, the prevailing theory is that it's rat meat. The cooks here are rather economical, and we do get large rats in the labyrinth—"

"What's Basilisk and Toadcurdle?" I interrupted. Rat-meat rumors could wait. I wanted to hear about those words.

"Societies," Tearly said. "You'll have to join one, everyone has to."

"And there's a labyrinth?"

"Girl," Tearly said. "You have so much to learn about this place."

We reached a set of stone steps. At the top was a door of solid wood, carved with intricate depictions of hoofed boys and winged girls and old women with snake bodies. It was the kind of thing you could get lost looking at—your eye kept finding new and startling things to focus on—but then Tearly was pulling on the dragon-shaped handle, and the door opened to admit us into a vast foyer with a round skylight of stained glass high above us.

"How many are there?" I asked. "Societies, I mean?"

My voice echoed in the foyer.

"There are six, three for boys and three for girls—well, anyone can join any of them, but there's a bit of a gender divide anyway. Toadcurdle for the oddest among us, Dewdrop for those who want to sit on the grass and have book picnics and eat cupcakes, Stormtongue for those who like to debate and conversate and put on plays, Flameforge for the valiant and clever who like exploring the wild woods and testing their mettle, and Basilisk and Briar for the evil students."

"Evil students?"

She waved a hand. "You know—the social climbers, the schemers, the political players. The rich snobs."

"Which are you in?" I asked. I was guessing she'd say Stormtongue.

Tearly rolled her eyes. "Ugh, I'm in Dewdrop—I was a nervous first year, and I had a crush on a student in that society. Of course, they didn't give me the time of day, and now they've graduated while I'm stuck with the ninnies." She glanced me over. "You look like you might enjoy Flameforge. Just a guess."

I liked the sound of cupcakes and book picnics, whatever that was, more than wild woods and mettle-testing, but I didn't argue with her assessment. "Which one was that again?" I wondered if I ought to be writing this down.

"Don't worry," Tearly said. "This will all be explained at orientation. And don't worry about Basilisk or Briar either, they're by invitation only, and they only invite the richest, snobbiest, most magic-blooded students of Spellwood."

She led me across the marble floor, smoothed by the passage of thousands of feet, to a wooden window in the far wall. An ancient woman stared down at us with a hawk-like gaze. She appeared human to my eyes until she reached out a hand for my letter of acceptance, and I saw that she had webbed fingers and nails like claws.

"I'll need your tears and a sample of laughter," she said as she took the letter from me and glanced it over. "And we will be collecting a drop of blood, a lock of hair, and a cutting of fingernail." She pushed a pair of ornate silver scissors and a sharpened knife across the table at me. "Do you require assistance?"

I took the knife and scissors gingerly. "I, ah, no thank you."

I snipped a piece of hair from the base of my neck and clipped my pinkie fingernail. The drop of blood frightened me most, but I didn't want to look like a coward in front of this severe fae woman, so I held my breath and pressed the tip of the knife to my finger as if I had been doing it all my life. A single, quivering bead of ruby red appeared on my skin, and the woman captured it with a tiny glass jar.

"What are these things for?" I dared to ask.

"Protection spells," the woman said, whisking them away. "Identification spells. Tracking spells."

She returned with a furled piece of paper and an ornate metal key. "Here is your room key, a map of the campus, and a list of your classes. You will find your uniforms and other essentials already in your room."

"I don't get to choose my own classes?" I said, surprised and a little disappointed.

"First-year middlings take the basic courses appropriate for their track," she said, and turned away.

I looked at Tearly. "Middlings?"

"Don't be offended," she whispered. "It means, well, average. But most of us are in the middling track."

I must have looked even more confused at that explanation, for she went on to say, "There are two tracks at Spellwood—the middling track and the elite track. Those who have exceptional powers or noble blood take the elite track, with its special courses on diplomacy and high magic. The rest of us mixed-bloods are in the middling track. We learn about fae culture and history, and how to resist glamours and charms, and basically how to stay safe and integrate well into fairy courts, should we choose to go that route."

Tearly received her room key and schedule, and then she joined me once more. She glanced at my paper.

"Oh," she said. "You're in North like me. Come on. I'll show you the way."

It turned out that Spellwood had four dormitories for its students—the North Tower, the East Wing, the Westerly Addition, and the Southern Wing. The East and South Wing branched off the main building where the classes were held, and the Westerly Addition was located across another jewel-green lawn, in a beautiful stone building with a dome for a roof. The North Tower was situated amid a vast, manicured garden. They were, Tearly explained, informally known as North, East, Westerly, and Southern.

"I like North best," Tearly confided as she led me down a flight of steps and outside once more. "I think it has the most picturesque setting, although it is farthest from the dining hall. Southern is best for food access, East is best for a quick walk to classes, and Westerly is best for, well, not getting caught sneaking out at night. It has a whole wall of windows that overlook the West Woods, and there's a window in the attic that doesn't lock."

"What is North best for?" I asked.

"Peace and quiet," she said with a grin. "It's nice and peaceful at the top of the tower. But if you like parties, someone is always having a get-together down in the gardens below. You can look out and see what everyone's doing, and decide if you want to join in. Quite handy. Besides that, it's the prettiest dorm."

We walked along a stretch of gravel that led straight as an arrow toward a spiraling stone tower. Moss-covered statues lined the walk on either side. Some of the statues depicted men and women posed in fighting stances, others were centaurs, dragons, and satyrs. A hedge ran behind the statues, creating a kind of natural wall, and the scent of roses filled the air.

"We're near the Briar—that's one of the snobby societies—house," Tearly explained. "All the societies have a place where they meet. Unfortunately, that means we'll see more than our fair share of Briar girls on this path. On the upside, though, Toadcurdle boys tend to avoid it because they don't want to run into Briars."

A few students strolled along the grounds, but for the most part, the school was still empty.

"A lot of students don't come back until tonight," Tearly told me as we passed a clump of giggling girls with short green hair and pointed ears, who otherwise looked perfectly human. "There's a school superstition about having good luck in the coming year if you arrive by moonlight, and besides, nothing starts until tomorrow anyway. Everything is decorated, and they put out lanterns. It's fun."

"Why didn't you come at night, then?"

Tearly shrugged. "Luck never seems to stick to me anyway, and I like to get here before it's crowded. Nice to have free run of the place before it's full to the brim with giddy first years—no offense—and snobby elites."

The high green hedges on either side of the path formed walls for outdoor rooms within the garden, and I caught glimpses of some of them as we passed. One had a lily pad-choked, square pond in the center, complete with a fountain with a statue of a winged boy pouring water from a basin. Another was filled with sundials of various heights and sizes.

A group of students emerged from one of the hedge-lined garden paths that intersected with ours. I caught a glimpse of a hulking male student as big as a bookshelf, a dark-skinned girl as beautiful as a supermodel, and a massive gray dog that looked like a wolf. I knew without Tearly's explanation that these were all elites. They exuded power and privilege.

"Students aren't allowed to bring pets," Tearly was saying in disapproval, but I barely heard her, because I was looking at the last student to step onto the path.

A boy.

He was lean and muscled like a panther, and he moved with the grace of one too. His face was angular, full of sharp lines along his jaw and cheekbones, and his hair was tousled midnight. He wore a blue cloak and clothing that looked as if it'd come from a renaissance faire—an open-necked shirt and loose trousers tucked into boots. He had a book under his arm, and he looked human except for what I realized with a start was curving horns sprouting from his temples, curling down around his forehead like a crown. No, not horns. Antlers. Small ones, so unobtrusive that I hadn't noticed them at first. They looked like a circlet of thorns almost. He was handsome in a dangerous, almost cruel way.

His eyes, green threaded with gold, landed on mine.

CHAPTER SEVEN

THE ANTLERED BOY'S bold stare pinned me to the ground. The wind blew suddenly, brushing his dark hair across his eyes, but he didn't move to brush it away. He seemed turned to stone at the sight of me.

My stomach twisted into a knot, and I felt like I couldn't breathe. Something about that look tugged at me in a dark, compelling way. For a moment that seemed to last for hours, I was stuck, unable to breathe, unable to tear my attention away.

"Kyra?" Tearly asked, breaking into my thoughts, and the rest of the world rushed in with color and sound.

The dark-haired, antlered boy was still staring at me. A scowl had twisted across his handsome face, and then the dog bumped his hand with its muzzle, and he snapped his gaze from mine. I breathed out, feeling as if I'd been released from knifepoint.

"Who are they?" I breathed, still unable to move away.

"That's Lucien and his friends," Tearly said. "The stunningly beautiful one is Selene. The big guy is Declan. They're friends with Isadora too."

Selene leaned over and whispered something in Lucien's ear, and he turned to look at us again. A scornful smirk crossed his lips, but when he looked at me, it faded, and his eyebrows drew together with obvious displeasure.

"The tower's this way," Tearly said, gesturing down another path through the hedges.

"Is there a reason why he's looking at me like I just pissed on his breakfast?" I muttered to Tearly.

"Come on," she said. "They're just... like that. They don't like anybody but themselves. Their coldness isn't your fault. Now, come on."

She drew me past the group of elites at a brisk walk, and I resisted the urge to look over my shoulder at them. I could feel Lucien's burning stare on my back all the rest of the way to the tower, and I felt woefully self-conscious. Had he looked at me and wondered what a human-looking student like me was doing here?

I frowned, a spurt of anger shooting through me. I had as much right as he did to attend the school, even if I didn't have webbed hands or pointed ears. I was still fae.

But a flicker of an insidious worry wormed its way through my stomach, and I couldn't get that piercing, scornful gaze out of my head.

What if whatever I was, wasn't enough for this place?

~

My room was located at the highest point of the North Tower.

"It's usually a first year's room," Tearly puffed as we climbed the spiraling staircase up and up and up. "And it's always a middling's. Sorry. It's a steep climb, as you can see, ha, so nobody elite wants it." She paused at a little landing where a stain glass window looked out over the gardens. "Most first years want to be in Westerly because of the aforementioned sneaking out stuff, and second years just want to be on the ground floor most of the

47

time. Third and fourth years just want to be in Southerly near the food. The elites get the biggest rooms in the best places, and most of them request to be in East so they can sleep in later before class. There aren't many elites in any of the other dormitories."

The mention of elites made me think of Lucien and his stare, and a nervous flutter went through my stomach. I shook my head, trying to banish the sensation.

What some snobby, handsome elite thought didn't matter to me. We'd probably never so much as speak to each other.

Tearly and I reached the top of the stairs, where we found a round landing and two doors set in the walls on opposite sides of the staircase. One had my room number on it. The other, only a symbol I didn't understand.

Tearly glanced at it and shrugged. "Supply closet, maybe."

I pulled out my room key and inserted it into the lock. The door swung open beneath my fingertips, revealing the room beyond.

I gasped.

A gabled room with a pale blue ceiling and smooth stone floors waited beyond. Three windows looked over the gardens in different directions, each window nestled in an arched recess. There was a soot-covered fireplace, and bookshelves covering the entirety of the wall that the door opened out of. The two of the other three walls had a bed—one a single and the other bunk beds. The walls were painted a pale, warm yellow.

"It's a bit small for three people," Tearly was saying apologetically. "But first years don't get the first choice—"

"I love it," I whispered, afraid to break the spell of this beautiful, homey, comfortable room.

A lump on the top bunk stirred, causing us both to jump in surprise. The blanket convulsed, and then a girl poked her head out from beneath it.

"Hello," she said, blinking at us. "Are you my new roommates?"

"Roommate," Tearly said, gesturing at me, and I waved.

"I'm Kyra," I said. "I'm a first-year student," I felt it necessary to add, lest she think me an idiot for not knowing anything at all.

"My name is Lyrica," my new roommate replied. "I'm a first year too." She slid out from beneath the blanket and jumped off the top of the bunk, and I tried my best not to stare, because she had wings.

Tiny, flimsy little wings. They were slightly furry, like moth wings, and they were a pale, mint green color. They protruded just beyond the tips of her shoulders, and they buzzed a little as she smiled nervously at me. Lyrica had sleek black hair and feathery-soft eyelashes. Her skin had the faintest sheen to it, as if she'd once been covered in glitter, and her skin still bore the phantom memory of it.

"I'm from the spring court," she said, looking me over curiously. "What about you? From where do you hail?"

"The, ah, summer court," I said, and instantly felt embarrassed. I felt like an imposter. I'd never even been to the summer court. It was hardly mine. "At least," I added, "that's where my father was from."

49

"Do you mean you... you grew up with mortals?" Lyrica asked with a gasp.

"Ah, yes. Sort of. My mom and grandmother are part-fae like me—"

But Lyrica was staring at me with wide eyes, as if I'd just admitted to being raised by zebras. "I've never met my father," she said. "I know his name was Gregory Choi, and I have this picture." She fumbled with a locket at her chest, opening it to a picture of a handsome Korean-American man with perfectly sculpted cheekbones. "But that's all. I've never been to the mortal world. I only have my mother's stories of it." She paused. "Is it true that you light cakes on fire to celebrate the day of your birth?"

"Um, well, sort of," I said. "We use candles."

"Oh," Lyrica said. She looked mildly disappointed. "Candles."

I looked at the other two beds. I could take the single bed by the window, or the bottom bunk beneath Lyrica.

I picked the single bed and set my leather bag on the mattress, and Lyrica perked up at the thought of something else.

"Is it true that you are carried everywhere in metal automatons that leak smoke into the air? Does it make it hard to breathe?" Lyrica asked, following me. "Does the air smell terrible? I should think it would make me feel faint to have vapors everywhere like that."

"Oh, well," I began uncertainly. I moved past her to peek through a door on the other end of the room. "We have cars. And pollution."

Lyrica followed me. "Pollution," she repeated. "Is that a type of spell?"

50

The door opened into a bathroom tiled in jade-green stones, with a giant, claw-footed tub and a sink and toilet that looked like they'd come from the 1920s. Sunlight spilled in through a round skylight overhead.

"And is it true that nobody has any tails or wings?" Lyrica added from the doorway, glancing me over as I turned to face her. "Do they all look like you?"

"Well," I stammered, thrown off-kilter by her relentless inquisitiveness. "People can look all kinds of ways. But no, no tails or wings."

Somewhere in the distance, a clock chimed the hour, the sound echoing.

"Fell's horses," Lyrica exclaimed. "What is that?"

"The bell," Tearly said. "I think this is where I make my exit. It's going to be dark soon, and I want to get the best bed before the rest of my roommates arrive. I'll see you around, Kyra. My room is on the first floor, the one right next to the stairs. Visit any time. And Lyrica?"

"Hmm?" Lyrica said, still studying me with hungry interest.

"Don't ask her too many questions. And answer some of hers too. She's never been to any of the fae courts."

Tearly disappeared, shutting the door behind her, and I was left alone with Lyrica, who gaped at me.

"Never?" she asked in astonishment.

"Never," I admitted. "And I've never met my father either."

She smiled at me in warm solidarity, looking at me less like I was a curiosity now, and more like I was a person in the same boat as her. I relaxed a little, returning her smile.

51

Maybe I was going to be okay here.

Lyrica continued to pepper me with questions while I found my uniforms hanging in the closet behind the door. The formal clothes were all maroon-colored robes that looked as if they'd come from the eleventh century, with drooping, bell-shaped sleeves and a belt of twisted gold. The after-hours clothing was similar, although they came in different shades of maroon. Slender, asymmetrical tunics, some sleeveless, some with flowing sleeves, and clinging, soft pants that felt more like leggings.

"I look terrible in the first-year colors," Lyrica muttered from where she'd climbed back into her bed. "My best color is silver. I can't wait to be a fourth year."

"Do the different years wear different colors?" I asked, still examining the clothing. Everything was my exact size.

"First years wear that fellish red," Lyrica said, blinking her feathery lashes at me. "Seconds wear brown. Third years are dark blue, and fourth years wear silver. If you stay on a fifth year or apprentice to become a teacher here, you wear yellow. Teachers wear black."

I looked back at my clothes. "What about what we wear to sleep?"

"Underthings and night clothes are in the drawers," Lyrica said with a wave of her hand. "I prefer to sleep naked, but..." She looked at me. "Would you prefer I didn't? I've heard mortals are less fond of nudity."

"Well," I said. "Er. At least not in common areas. If it isn't too much trouble?"

"I can act like a mortal," Lyrica said with a grin. "It feels so delightfully authentic."

I spotted trunks sitting beneath the beds. I found one with my name on it and looked inside. Plain, sturdy underwear, nightgowns, and more soft legging-pants, all in the various shades of maroon. There were two bras, but they looked a bit more like soft corsets, the kind of thing someone from the nineteenth century might wear. I examined them curiously.

"We do get to wear whatever we want to the balls and on holidays, at least," Lyrica said then. "That's nice. I'm planning on wearing a silver and violet gown to the Summertide celebration. What are you going to wear?"

Before I could answer, the door opened, and our third roommate stepped into the room.

CHAPTER EIGHT

OUR THIRD ROOMMATE introduced herself as Hannah Harris, and she was as blatantly and unremarkably human as I was. She was tiny, with curly yellow hair, an adorably slightly upturned nose, and a stubborn, almost aggressive tilt to her chin that suggested she'd been fighting against being called "cute" for most of her life. She was also a first year, and although she'd lived most of her life in the mortal realm, she had often visited her fae relatives at the autumnal court. Her only fae connection was a great-great great grandfather who'd had golden hair, eyes, and skin. The only thing she'd inherited from him was her hair, she noted with a sigh of regret.

"How many courts are there?" I finally demanded, and both Hannah and Lyrica looked at me like I'd asked what water was.

"Seven," Hannah answered. "The favorite number of the fae." She ticked the names off her fingers one by one. "The summer court, the winter court, the spring and autumnal courts, the sun court, the water court, and the dark court. Sometimes the sun court is called the fire court, and the dark court is also called the moon court or the night court."

"Do the names describe them? Is it... always spring in the spring court, for instance, and always night in the dark court?" I asked. I felt foolishly ignorant now.

"Well, no," Hannah said. "But also, well, yes. Sort of. The kingdom—the fae kingdom, I mean—has seasons like the mortal realm. But the courts have more power during their respective phases. The spring court flourishes and has its greatest surge of power in spring, for instance. The dark court is more powerful at night. The water court is always powerful, but they are limited to their borders of rivers and sea. And so forth. There have been wars between the light and the dark, the seelie and unseelie," she added, "particularly between the sun court and the dark court, which are the most powerful, but there is peace now."

What she lacked in fae blood, it seemed, Hannah made up for in knowledge. I was glad she was my roommate.

After we'd all chosen our beds and explored our wardrobes, we put on our maroon after-hours clothing and went together to eat dinner in the dining hall. I was itching to try out the function of the locket my mom and Grandmother Azalea had given me, to send a message to them that I was safe and happy, but I was starving.

I'd send the message tonight.

The paths in the garden were more crowded now, although nobody else seemed to be wearing their uniforms yet.

"Perhaps putting on the uniforms was a rookie mistake," Hannah murmured as we stood in line to enter the dining facilities. "We look like first years."

"We *are* first years," Lyrica said in confusion.

"Yes, but we don't want to look like it, do we?" Hannah replied.

"Why ever not?" Lyrica asked.

The dining room had a great, arching ceiling that was covered in thick green vines heavy with lush foliage. Lanterns dangled from among them, casting a warm glow across the wooden tables and benches, and blossoms bloomed among the leaves. I craned my neck, staring in awe. It was beautiful.

As I was looking upward, I took a step forward into what had been an empty space devoid of any other people, and ran into something hard and muscled.

A chest.

I snapped my gaze from the ceiling, and my eyes landed on the playfully smirking face of a student with bronzed-brown skin, flowing golden hair that brushed his powerful shoulders, and yellow-brown eyes. He was handsome, and he obviously knew it.

"Hello," the student said, catching me by the elbow as I stumbled. He unleashed a dimpled smile on me, making my stomach flip.

"I'm sorry," I stammered. "I was looking at the ceiling. I didn't mean to run into you."

"It's beautiful," he agreed, but he was looking at my face instead of upward as he spoke the words. His smile deepened, and so did his dimples.

I flushed at the intensity of his attention. Was he flirting with me specifically, or was he the kind of guy who did that with everyone? I didn't want to assume and make a fool of myself. "My name is Kyra Solschild," I said, feeling awkward and charmed at the same time.

"Griffin," he introduced himself. He still hadn't let go of my elbow. "Third year, elite. You must be a first year. I've never seen you before, and I would have noticed you. What court is your family from?"

"The summer court," I said, managing not to stammer this time.

His eyebrows lifted. "The summer court? I hail from the sun court, closest friends with the summer court. But I do not know you."

"I grew up in the mortal realm," I explained quickly. "And I, er, this is Lyrica and Hannah," I said, gesturing vaguely at my roommates, who were gaping at Griffin as if he had three heads.

Griffin nodded at them politely and then returned his bright gaze to me again. His lips curved in another smile, this one inviting.

"Would you like to eat with me?" he asked.

Tearly's earlier admonition to stay away from elites ran through my head. I'd just gotten here. I had been counting on the companionship and solidarity of Lyrica and Hannah while I fumbled my way through my first meal here. I didn't want to try to navigate through the unfamiliarity while under the gaze of this bronzed demigod, no matter how good-looking or charming he was.

"Maybe another time?" I said. "I was planning on eating with my friends tonight."

Griffin's brow wrinkled with astonishment, and he appeared genuinely flummoxed, as if he'd never been told no before. "Oh. I suppose—"

"Thank you," I added, and then I grabbed Lyrica and Hannah and rushed past him toward the tables in the center of the room where the food was laid out like a sumptuous feast. There were whole roasted game hens—at least, I thought they were hens—and piles of fruits, and fire-browned bread spilling out of baskets.

I would have stared longer at the delicious-looking food, but my attention was snagged by a group sitting a few tables over, close enough that they'd undoubtedly just witnessed the interaction between Griffin and me.

The elites from earlier, the ones with the big dog—Selene, Declan, and Lucien. The dog wasn't with

57

them now, but Isadora was, as well as another male student with dark red hair and a foxlike smile.

Lucien was glowering at me. He had one hand braced on the table as if holding himself in place, and the other was clenched around a book in his lap. He looked furious.

Was he mad that I was talking to another elite? Did he think it beneath me, a middling first year?

I turned my back on him, pretending I didn't feel uneasy at his hostility.

"Kyra!" Lyrica gasped as we picked up plates and served ourselves food. "He asked you to eat with him, and you told him no?"

"I don't even know him," I whispered, putting a generous slice of bread onto my plate as I forced myself not to look back over my shoulder at Lucien and his scowl. It was unnerving, but I wouldn't let it get to me.

"That was Griffin, grandson of King Alondicus and one of the princes of the sun court," Hannah said. She had a stunned expression on her face. "I don't think anyone has ever refused him before."

"Well, it's probably a good learning experience for him, then." I grabbed a few apples, a serving of the meat, and a dish of a quivering substance that looked like pudding. I was embarrassed now—embarrassed at my earlier panic, and a little defensive of my choice. "He isn't really my type. I don't want to give him the idea that I'm interested…"

"Not your type?" Lyrica looked scandalized. "A prince is everyone's type. Well, I suppose unless your type is princesses, or royals of a neutral gender—"

"I like princes," I interrupted. "Well, I mean, guys. But more, you know, the dark-haired, bookish kind." I flushed as I realized I'd described Lucien, who most certainly wasn't my type. "I mean, the humble, nerdy type. The kind who like to hang out in coffee shops and libraries. Griffin looks like..." *The sun in human form,* I wanted to say. "He looks like he's used to golden palaces and caviar. His family wouldn't like me. I'm too human for him."

"Don't sell yourself short," Hannah said, her eyes flashing with sudden fire. "You deserve to be here, and so do I."

I got the impression she said that a lot to people.

"I just want to get settled," I said. "Get my bearings."

We found a table and sat down, and I immediately stuffed bread in my mouth for an excuse to stop talking.

"Well," Lyrica said around a bite of her food. "If he's looking for a girl to take to the Wintertide ball and you turn him down, tell him I am interested." She glanced at Hannah. "What about you? Shall we duel for him?"

"I'm not here to meet anybody either," Hannah said resolutely. "I don't want to get distracted from my studies and goals. He's all yours." She popped a grape into her mouth.

Lyrica sighed. "Well, he's hardly that. But thanks. I'd have to tell my betrothed anyway."

"Your... betrothed?" I asked.

She shrugged one slender shoulder. "I am engaged to be married to a fae boy from the summer court following my studies here at Spellwood. Until then, we have an arrangement. I can see whomever I like, and so can he. It only seems fair."

"An open relationship?" Hannah supplied.

"Yes." Lyrica leaned her cheek on one hand and plucked at her dinner with the other. "It was my idea."

"Is he not here?" I asked.

"He is full-blooded fae," she said, not sounding particularly enthusiastic. "And it wasn't my idea to marry him, either, but he's nice enough. It's a good match for our families. His name is Alcorn."

"Alcorn!" Hannah exclaimed. "I know him."

Lyrica lifted an eyebrow as if to say, *you see?*

Hannah made a face. "He's nice, like you said. A good, solid fellow. A little..."

"Odd?" Lyrica said.

"He's eccentric," Hannah agreed. "But nice. He truly is."

A silver-haired woman dressed in light purple serving robes with black stripes across the neck and hem stopped at our table to bring us drinks in heavy wooden goblets. Her face wore a faraway expression, and her hands were slow and dreamy as she handed set down the cups. I stared at her, torn between confusion and concern. After she glided away, I looked at Lyrica and Hannah to see if they'd noticed her odd behavior.

They were both eating as if nothing were wrong.

"Our server seemed... unwell," I said.

"Oh," Lyrica said. "She's just charmed. Don't worry."

"Charmed?" I stole a glance over my shoulder.

"Some of the servants and custodial staff here at Spellwood are serving a sentence or repaying a debt to fae society," Hannah explained. "It's a common means of restitution among the courts. Lawbreakers are given a choice, usually. They can work here under a charm for safety, or sit in the court's dungeon. They are charmed to keep them orderly and to ensure they are not a danger to the students. The ones serving a sentence have the black stripe on their purple uniforms."

I stared at her in horror. "They're... slaves?"

"No, no, it's like community service in the mortal realm," Hannah said. "And it's a light sentence. Some courts punish especially bad behavior by cutting off ears or turning the offenders into toads for a year. Or execution. This is useful, and they are treated with dignity. They know where they are, but they cannot interact with us."

I still felt weird and unsettled about it. "Are all of the staff charmed prisoners?"

"No," Hannah said, shaking her curly hair. "Most are former students who live and work here fulltime now. Half-bloods with nowhere to go."

I stole a few glances at Lucien and his friends while I ate. He was ignoring me now, reading from the book that had been in his lap. Whatever thought had made him so furious earlier seemed to have abated.

Still, I didn't understand why he seemed to have such an issue with me.

"What do you know about them?" I asked, nodding at the table of elites.

Hannah made a sound of disgust. "The red-haired one is Tryst, from the autumnal court. He's a first year like us, but he's an elite. He won't have any classes with us." Judging by her tone, they weren't friends. "The dark-haired one is Lucien. He's a second-year student."

"He's from the dark court," Lyrica added. "Fell's bells, he's handsome, isn't he?"

"And he's Griffin's half-brother," Hannah said.

61

Half-brother? Maybe that was why he was so angry. He didn't approve of his brother slumming with a middling girl who was barely fae. A pang of burning shame pierced my chest, and my fears of inadequacy whispered in my ears. I pushed them away. Like Hannah said, I deserved to be here too.

"How is he from the dark court if Griffin's from the sun court? If they're brothers?" I asked. The mechanics of it all was still fresh and confusing to me.

Aren't those courts mortal enemies?"

"*Half*-brothers," Lyrica emphasized.

"His father had a fling with a half-mortal princess of the dark court and conceived a child—Lucien—while his wife, Lindraia, was recovering from the birth of Griffin," Hannah said. "Somehow, he didn't die, even though he was of both sun and night blood. His mere existence was a great scandal for many years, and they say his father's wife still refuses to even speak Lucien's name. He and Griffin did not grow up together, of course. They only interacted when Griffin and his father visited the dark court, and Lucien grew up in disgrace."

How oddly tragic, I thought.

"Don't feel too sorry for him," Hannah said, reading my expression. "He's rich and spoiled. He is still a prince, even if he is an unwanted one. And he has the worst taste in friends."

I stole another glance at the table. At Selene, dark and beautiful, Isadora, her black eyes slitted in some private anger at Declan, who, I realized, had a tail. Tryst lolled in his chair, smirking at them all.

They looked like the pinnacle of snobby, rich students at the top of Spellwood's food chain, the kind that were too beautiful and privileged for their own good.

"What societies are they in?"

"Basilisk, I bet," Hannah said with a sigh. "Maybe the girls are in Briar. Let's talk about something else, please? Something that doesn't churn my stomach."

"I heard," Lyrica said, wide-eyed, "There was once a seventh society called Ghostbellow, but then they all disappeared. Though I've heard they still exist, they're just all ghosts now—"

"Oh, that's just a rumor spread by Toadcurdle back when my father was a student at Spellwood," Hannah declared with a wave of her hand. "It isn't true. He said they made it up so they could blame their pranks on someone else."

They broke into a spirited argument over the origin of Hannah's facts and the veracity of Lyrica's, but I was no longer listening. I was still looking at Lucien.

He always seemed to be reading a book.

Before I could turn back to our dinner, Lucien's eyes slid from his book and caught mine again, and a shiver passed through me at the intensity in his dark gaze.

What did he want? Why did he keep looking at me like that?

I turned my head, breaking the stare, feeling somehow like I'd lost in a contest of wills.

CHAPTER NINE

ORIENTATION TOOK PLACE the next morning at nine o'clock. Hannah, Lyrica, and I woke groggy and late for breakfast, for we had stayed up late into the night telling stories of our childhoods and getting to know each other. I felt like death warmed over, for after the other girls had fallen asleep, I'd tested my locket with a scrap of paper that said simply, *miss you*. I'd sat up waiting for the reply until nearly morning, when I'd fallen asleep with the locket still clutched in my hand.

In the morning light, the scrap of paper inside the locket read, *Miss you too.*

Tears flooded my eyes, and I stared at the paper until the chiming of the clock outside broke into my thoughts, reminding me of the time. I only had time to scrub myself over with a washcloth wet in the sink of our bathroom, brush my teeth, and throw on my uniform before I joined the others scrambling down the spiral staircase.

Lyrica was somewhat fuzzy on concepts of hours and minutes. Hannah and I, being familiar with the mortal realm, had to explain three times what nine o'clock actually meant while we scrambled up the path toward the dining hall in our new maroon robes. I felt a little bit like I was going to be an extra on the set of a movie. I'd left my hair down long because I hadn't liked the look of it in a ponytail with the formal robes, and it was flowy and messy because I hadn't had time to do anything with it.

"How do you tell time in your court?" Hannah was asking Lyrica in an attempt to find a suitable analogy for the fae girl's mind to make sense of.

"We might say, meet me when the dew sparkles on the lawn," she replied, blinking her feathery lashes as if this were the most sensible thing in the world. "Or, the party will begin when the first star glistens in the evening sky. Or, wake when the spiders finish their webs."

"But what if you don't know when that will be?" I asked. "Do you have to get up and feel the ground to see if it's wet enough? How can you plan around that kind of imprecision?"

"You just... know," Lyrica insisted. "It's like a tug in your chest. The spring court is in tune with the world around it. We breathe in time with it, you see. It's in our blood and bones."

"What about your court?" I asked Hannah.

"The autumnal court uses sundials like proper folk," Hannah said.

In Spellwood Academy, the use of clocks was apparently a concession to the more mortal of the students. A way to keep everyone on the same page, as it were. I was deeply grateful. If I had to be punctual based on things like sparkling dew and first stars, I'd be late to every class. And I certainly didn't want to tell time based on anything having to do with spiders.

After breakfast, the entire student body gathered in the main assembly hall. It was an echoing chamber made of stone, with arching windows soaring high above our heads and letting in streams of golden sunlight. The students sat on wooden steps that descended downward in a circle.

The headmaster, a tall and strong-looking woman with feathered wings of white and a crown of silver braids, addressed us. Her name was Headmaster Atalara Windswallow, she said, and she'd been headmaster of the academy for more than half a century, even though she didn't look nearly old enough for that.

"Students," she said, her voice ringing like a trumpet, cutting through the whispers and giggles and rendering the room utterly silent and at attention. "Welcome to a new year at Spellwood Academy."

A swell of excitement swept through the room. Even the jaded fourth years seemed to feel it. Most of the first years broke out in excited applause, a few of them cheering before the teachers hushed them so the headmaster could continue.

Much of her speech was things I'd already heard yesterday from Tearly—the four dormitories and their locations, the societies' names, the fact that we'd all be required to join one. She also directed our attention to a student rulebook, which, she explained, each student had a copy of in their room. She reviewed a few of the rules, some the kind you'd hear at every school, like no fighting, no stealing, no cheating... and some, well, not. There was to be no use of charms or magic without permission during the semester, with the exception of the society night and certain celebrations, and then only for dramatic effect and decoration. There were to be no hexes, no curses, and no communication with the outside world except through the proper channels, mainly letters, which could be scanned for charms and hexes. The whole campus, she explained, was bounded by spells for safety, and any spells or charms performed within the boundaries were detectable by the professors.

Apparently, security was an issue of genuine concern. My mom had been right. I would be protected here.

I thought more of my mom and Grandmother Azalea as I reached for the locket around my neck. Was that an improper channel? I didn't want to ask and have the locket taken away. If I used it, would they know?

The headmaster had mentioned letters. I would write to them that way just in case, and leave the locket for emergencies.

Headmaster Windswallow was explaining the use of clocks to tell time to some of the more fae among us when my attention wandered a little. I turned my head to look around me, and caught the eye of Tearly, sitting a few rows back. She grinned at me and flicked her fingers in a wave. I smiled back. Then my gaze shifted, and my smile faltered.

A few rows behind her sat Lucien and his crew. They hadn't seen me, and I took the opportunity to study the disgraced prince of the dark court.

He was handsome, I had to admit. Today, his hair curled in unruly waves over and around his crown of antlers, making them almost invisible. I noticed that his ears were slightly pointed at the ends. He was still holding a book, a different one this time.

I was trying to read the name on the spine when he turned his head and caught me looking.

Heat rushed through my cheeks and flamed across my throat. Lucien's mouth twitched once in what might have been a smirk before I whirled back around, my heart slamming.

Why had I been looking at him like that? So openly? Now he probably thought I was some besotted idiot when I'd just wanted to know the name of his damn book.

My ears were still burning when Headmaster Windswallow finished her speech and dismissed us to lunch. Classes, we were informed, began promptly at one o'clock, and the society night would be in several weeks' time. A more specific measurement was quoted—something about fortnights and crescent moons—but I wasn't sure how it translated, timewise.

"I'll never figure this clock stuff out," Lyrica said mournfully as we filed toward the dining hall. "I'll be perpetually lost."

"One o'clock is when... ah, when the sun is a waltz away from high noon," Hannah tried, which didn't make sense to me at all.

Lyrica brightened. "Well, fell's feathers, why didn't she just say that?"

"I don't understand the way the days and weeks are measured here," I said. "Days, yes, and weeks, but what about all this other stuff? Moons and things."

"A moon cycle is a month," Hannah said. "The school observes time like mortals do, but old habits... you know."

I sighed.

Lunch was composed of big black pots of soup, some of them cool and mint-scented, others bubbling hot. One had what looked like an eyeball floating in it.

"Toad's eye stew!" Lyrica squealed. "My favorite!"

"The eyes give it a special flavor," Hannah explained to me as she saw my hesitation. "But nobody eats them."

"Speak for yourself," Lyrica said as she ladled a giant serving of eyeballs into a bowl.

I looked away before I could gag at the sight, and I spotted another familiar face.

Griffin.

He sat at a nearby table, surrounded by other elites. He looked resplendent in his school uniform, and his tawny-gold eyes gleamed as he looked me over and then winked.

My stomach twisted nervously. I wasn't sure what to do with such naked admiration. It was flattering, but unnerving.

After I nodded back, Griffin rose and strolled over.

Up close, he smelled like heated bronze and sunbaked apples, and I had the faint feeling of standing close to a warm fire. "So, we meet again."

"Yes. Um. Hi."

A lazy smile tipped the corners of his mouth. "Come sit with me."

"I..." I stole a glance at Lyrica and Hannah, who nodded at me. "Er, yes. Fine. I will."

The force of Griffin's full smile was like the flash of sunlight on water—blinding.

I grabbed my bowl of soup and followed him back to his table. As I found my seat, I nearly dropped one of the bowls, and Griffin lay a steadying hand on my shoulder. His fingers were almost scorching hot.

I sat.

The others at the table looked at me curiously. Their faces were not particularly welcoming, but not malicious either. They seemed more confused at my inclusion than anything else, as if they weren't sure why Griffin had asked me to join them. I was obviously more mortal than fae, and obviously middling.

Everyone else at the table, if I had to bet, was an elite. I'd stake a good amount of money on it.

Three girls with violet hair who appeared to be triplets stared at me from either side of Griffin as he settled himself on the bench opposite me. Beyond them sat a young man with a horn growing out of the center of his forehead like a rhinoceros. He was big and brawny, and his hands looked like they could crush small rocks, but his gray eyes were soft.

"Sylla, Nylla, Merit, and Bigs," Griffin introduced them with a wave of his hand. "This is Kyra."

"What court are you from?" one of the triplets—Nylla?—asked me. Her gaze flicked over my maroon robes, and she lifted an eyebrow.

"The summer court," I said.

This appeared to surprise them all.

"I've never seen you before," the other of the triplets—Sylla?—said. "Unless... are you that mortal girl who drank too much honeysuckle wine and almost drowned in the crescent lake last year?"

"I've never been to the summer court," I admitted. "I grew up in the mortal realm."

For a second, they looked as if I'd said I drank my own urine, but they all quickly covered their surprise and disgust and smiled at me again.

"What society are you planning to join?" Griffin asked, impervious to his friends' reactions.

"I haven't decided yet," I said, which was true. Even if I had, I didn't feel like trotting my choice out

70

for his friends to scorn behind their fake smiles. "What society are you all in?"

I was almost certain what their answers would be.

"Basilisk," Bigs said as if I'd asked the color of the sky. "The girls are in Briar."

I nodded as though this were a revelation to me.

"You could join Briar," Griffin said. "They'd be happy to have you."

I didn't miss the way the girls' eyes narrowed, but they didn't contradict his statement.

"Oh, she probably wants to join Dewdrop," one of the girls said quickly, snickering under her breath.

Now I was truly annoyed. So much for keeping quiet about my choices.

"I was thinking Flameforge," I said, mostly because it seemed like an impressive society, and I didn't miss the flicker of amusement that crossed one of the triplet's face. As if she didn't think I could get in.

"Flameforge is a respectable society," Griffin said. "But you'll have to pass their trials if you want to be accepted. Briar is better."

"Do you think I can?" I asked, fluttering my eyelashes at him mostly because I wanted to see that look of disgust on the triplets' faces again. Maybe if I thought of it as funny rather than humiliating, I wouldn't feel so trampled upon.

Griffin seemed pleased that I was asking his opinion. "I think," he said, capturing my hand and holding it in his own as he looked into my eyes, "that you can do whatever you set your mind to. You seem like a strong woman."

"Thank you, Griffin," I said, smiling at him.

He beamed and pressed a kiss to the back of my hand. The resulting frowns from Bigs and the triplets was more rewarding than I'd anticipated.

~

At one o'clock, I rushed with Hannah to our first class. We had the same schedule, being as we were both mostly mortal and fully middling.

I could tell that Hannah resented the fact that she had to take what was essentially remedial fae courses, but she bravely pretended she wasn't.

Our first class was called Middle Histories of the Folk. There was also, apparently, an Ancient Histories of the Folk and a Modern Histories of the Folk, but Middle seemed to be the place to start. Hannah whispered to me as we entered the classroom that the Middle History was the most relevant when it came to building a historical foundation for the current arrangement of kingdoms and politics.

As I entered the room, I was startled to see Selene, one of Lucien's crew, half-reclining gracefully in one of the seats. She was dressed in her year's colors and obviously wasn't a middling student. Her gaze passed over me coolly as I entered. I took a seat as far away from her as possible. In my distraction, I bumped into another student, a girl with hair in three braids down her back interwoven with thorns and brambles. She whirled on me with her razor-sharp teeth bared in a snarl.

"Watch it," she hissed, flicking a forked tongue at me.

"Sorry." I took a step back and felt Hannah grab my elbow.

"She's from one of the unseelie courts, no doubt," Hannah murmured in my ear. "Most of us don't care where the rest are from, but there's always a few of what are called Warmongers, those who still take to heart the old feuds and wars. Unseelie versus Seelie. And some of them have short tempers, so avoid them if you can."

Our teacher, whose name was Professor Quaddlebush, was a small man with wings on his back and a pair of spectacles that didn't seem to want to stay on the bridge of his nose. He shoved the spectacles in place as he looked us over, and he introduced Selene as a special guest speaker on the first topic of the day, as apparently her great-great-grandfather had recorded the Middle Histories as we knew them.

That explained that mystery.

Then, Professor Quaddlebush asked us to each stand and give our names and respective courts one at a time.

My stomach twisted into yet another knot. Nervous anticipation was making my hands shake. The confrontation with the forked-tongued girl hadn't helped, either. My adrenaline burned through my arms and made me feel dizzy.

When it came time for me to give my name and court origin, I stood slowly and nervously turned to face the room. I felt the weight of their eyes on me.

"I'm Kyra," I said. "And, ah, I'm from the summer court."

"The shit court, more like it," the girl with the forked tongue said loud enough for everyone around us to hear.

My fear turned to fury as I snapped my gaze to hers. She was smirking at me.

Before I could open my mouth to snap back a response, however, her smirk turned to a gasp, and she made a strangled sound. Her face took on a greenish tint.

I stared. Was she choking? My anger bled away, and I stretched out a hand toward her. I knew CPR. I'd learned it in a lifeguarding class. Maybe—?

"Kyra!" Professor Quaddlebush shouted. "Stop at once! Stop, I say!"

I didn't understand what he was saying, but then the girl's face flattened and stretched, and I realized she was turning into a frog.

I gasped sharply, and my eyes landed on Selene, sitting a few rows away, laughing silently.

"Stop!" I cried, and the girl's face sagged, one eye bulbous and drooping. She put her hands up to cover herself as some of the students giggled, but most of them looked as shocked as I felt.

Why had Selene done that?

"Kyra," Professor Quaddlebush said, his voice brimming with badly-contained fury. "Using spells on other students is expressly forbidden, and will be punished swiftly and severely. Go at once to the headmaster's office."

CHAPTER TEN

"GO IMMEDIATELY TO see the headmaster," the professor bellowed as I stood transfixed with shock.

"But... I didn't..." I shot another look at Selene, who was smirking now. "I didn't do it. I don't know any spells."

"You stood there and pointed your hand at her, young lass. Don't try to lie to me."

"I—" I began again, feeling utterly helpless. I realized that this looked bad, but he had to listen to me.

Professor Quaddlebush did not seem to share my perspective on listening.

"At once!" the professor thundered, his tiny wings buzzing with emphasis.

I left my seat and exited the room, my heart slamming in my chest.

I didn't even know how to find the headmaster's office. I paced down the wide corridor, which was lined with windows overlooking the lawns outside. I passed doors to other classrooms, and inside, I could hear the droning of teacher voices, sometimes in other languages.

I reached an intersection of two hallways and stopped in surprise.

There, standing in the middle of the two hallways, was Lucien.

He looked like a prince from some ancient, otherworldly tragedy. His robes somehow managed to look majestic on him, and they had a sobering effect on his appearance. Instead of insolent, he looked regal.

And he looked unhappy to see me. His brows drew together, and his lips curved in a scowl.

"I'm looking for the headmaster's office," I stammered, doing my best not to cower beneath that angry expression.

He looked at me and didn't reply. One of his eyebrows lifted slightly.

Just then, the headmaster appeared in the corridor behind him.

"There you are," she said. "Both of you. Come."

Both of us?

Lucian turned and stalked in her direction with a kind of grim defiance. I followed, wondering what he'd done to get sent to the headmaster. Whatever it was, though, I had no doubt he was guilty of his accused crime.

We followed Headmaster Windswallow up a winding staircase that smelled like wax polish and sandalwood, past stern portraits of what I could only assume were the previous headmasters. The tips of Headmaster Windswallow's snowy white wings brushed the stairs as she climbed them, making a whispering sound against the polished wood. Somewhere, I could hear a clock ticking ominously.

We reached the top. Headmaster Windswallow's office turned out to be in a hexagon-shaped tower with windows that overlooked every direction of the Spellwood grounds.

She took her place behind an enormous desk and gestured at a stone bench against the wall. "Sit," she commanded.

We sat. Rather, I sat. Lucien draped himself across his half of the bench as if he didn't have a care in the world. He hadn't looked at me since the hallway, but kept his face resolutely fixed on the headmaster.

"Who wants to go first?" Headmaster Windswallow asked.

When neither of us answered, she brought her attention to bear on Lucien.

"Drop your glamour, if you please," she said firmly.

His glamour? I glanced at him, startled.

Lucien shifted on the bench. He sighed, his green eyes glittering angrily. As I watched, his face shimmered and shifted, the perfect smoothness of his sharp cheekbones melting away to reveal dark purple bruises across his jaw and temple, a deep cut above his left eyebrow, and a split lower lip.

"Fighting," Headmaster Windswallow said, "is expressly forbidden. Do you want to tell me why you were quarreling with another student, Lucien?"

"I do not," Lucien said stiffly. He still wouldn't look at me. He kept his eyes focused on the headmaster and his chin was now lifted in a stubborn attempt at dignity.

"That is your choice, but if you choose to remain silent, then I will double your punishment," she said, and waited.

Lucien still didn't speak.

Headmaster Windswallow tilted her head thoughtfully. "Well, then. The earthnyms seem to have exploded in population over the last few weeks, and they've taken to dancing in the Cistern at night. The stone is covered in moss and will have to be scraped clean. Six weeks, Lucien, every night following the dinner meal until the twilight hour, and absolutely no charms to lessen the labor."

I wasn't sure if it was a harsh sentence or not. At least, I supposed, she hadn't turned him into a frog or sent him home.

"And," the headmaster added, with a note of compassion in her voice. "I will allow the glamour until you see the healers."

Lucien nodded. He rose and stepped toward the door as the headmaster turned her attention to me.

"Kyra," she said. "I must confess I wasn't expecting this from you."

She spoke as if she knew things about me. I wondered what she could possibly know. What my bottled laugh and the lock of my hair might have conveyed to the school. Could they read things in the drop of my blood?

A bird that I hadn't noticed until that moment fluttered forward from where it had been perched on the windowsill, a curl of paper clutched in its beak.

I heard Lucien hesitate in the doorway.

Headmaster Windswallow took the paper from the bird, unfurled it, and read the message. She lifted her head and fixed her gaze on me. Her frown made me want to shrivel.

"Turned another student into a toad for taunting you, did you? Charms and spells are not allowed on campus, Kyra, and the punishment for employing them against a fellow student is severe."

"I actually didn't—" I tried to say, but she silenced me with a look.

"As you are a new student, and there was no actual harm done, I will be gracious this time. You will join Lucien in clearing the Cistern. Every night for six weeks. After the dinner meal until the twilight hour. And no charms, Kyra."

"I—"

"You are dismissed," she said.

Lucien was already gone by the time I reached the door.

CHAPTER ELEVEN

I WAS MOROSE at dinner in anticipation of my first round of punishment. Hannah, Lyrica, and Tearly, who'd joined us for the meal, all tried to bolster my spirits, but I felt like I was preparing to go to my execution as I picked at my food and tried not to look in the direction of Lucien and his cruel friends.

"How big is the Cistern?" I asked. "Is it... I mean, will we have to spend much time near each other?"

"The Cistern is an amphitheater," Tearly said. "Shaped like, well, a cistern. It's made from chiseled stone, and its nearly as ancient as the rocks its carved from."

"What are earthnyms?" I asked, desperate to distract myself in the last few moments before my punishment commenced.

"They're funny little things," Tearly said. "They look like the mortal idea of fairies—little things with wings—but they don't speak or have much comprehension of anything. They like to dance all night long, and they make toadstools and moss grow where their feet have touched the ground. My aunt had a nym infestation once. It was a dreadful problem."

"Wonderful," I muttered.

"But easily fixed!" Tearly hastened to say as she realized this wasn't helping.

When I could delay no longer, for most of the room had cleared, I rose to my feet and looked toward the exit.

"I suppose I should get to it," I said grimly.

The others walked me to the Cistern. The amphitheater lay on the far east side of the grounds, set in a hill like a giant's soup bowl that had been set down after dinner and forgotten. Stone levels descended toward a flat stage, the levels serving both as steps and seating. The stones were green with moss.

I groaned aloud at the sight of it.

This would take months to clear.

There was no sign of Lucien. I wondered if he was even going to bother to show up, and my spirits lifted slightly at the thought of being spared his glowering presence, even if it meant doing all the work myself.

A man, slightly stooped, approached us. I hadn't even noticed him standing there. He had green eyes, greenish lips, and green hair with tendrils of vines growing out from among his curls. He looked young and ancient at the same time.

"I'm Gallis," he said. "The groundskeeper. Here are your instruments for clearing the moss."

I was expecting something magical, something distinctly fae, like a tree branch magically twisted into some fantastic shape, but Gallis merely handed me a shovel and a hoe.

There was still no sign of Lucien. Had he decided to skip the punishment altogether?

Anger licked at my core despite my earlier relief at the thought of not having to see him. Did he think he was immune to the rules? How dare he flaunt his elite status? How dare he shrug off punishment?

Well, regardless of what Lucien was doing, I was here and this was my punishment. I heaved a sigh and used the shovel to scrape at the moss, but it clung as stubbornly to the rock beneath as if it were glued in place. I pried at a clump with the tip of the shovel, and the moss lifted slightly, root tendrils stretching from where they had melded with the stone ground beneath. I leaned hard on the shovel and heard a loud popping sound, and the moss came free and smacked me in the face.

I heard a snort of what might have been laughter. I turned and saw Lucien, his back to me, a hoe in hand. He appeared to be clearing the moss with no problem. He must be using magic despite Headmaster Windswallow's rules on the matter.

I scowled and redoubled my efforts. I would not let a spoiled fae prince show me up. I was strong. I could do this.

Sweat beaded on my forehead and trickled into my eyes as I worked, and a fine dusting of grit and bits of moss coated my arms before long. I fell into an exhausted rhythm—wedge the shovel tip beneath the moss, fill my lungs with the deepest breath I could inhale, throw my entire body weight onto the shovel's handle and strain to wrench the roots away from the rocks, and dodge the clumps of moss as they flew upward from the force of my efforts. Wedge, strain, dodge. Over and over until my shoulders, back, and arms ached and trembled, and I was soaked in perspiration and covered in dirt.

Every time I glanced over my shoulder at Lucien, he was ignoring me entirely. A blessing, I supposed. It was better than being taunted or glared at.

Still, his utter lack of acknowledgment rankled me. We were co-laborers in punishment, even though he deserved his sentence and I did not deserve mine. It could have given us something in common, perhaps. A moment of solidarity between middling and elite.

But Lucien acted as though I didn't exist.

The hours crawled past.

Finally, the sun sank below the tree line, and the first stars appeared in the purple twilight. Lucien laid down his tools and set off for the path toward the school without a backward glance.

Gallis appeared from the fragrant green shadows and held out his hand for my shovel. His nails, I noticed, were rough and brown, like bark.

I put it in his hands and turned to pick up the hoe. At least I'd cleared a good swath of—

I froze, staring in dismay.

Almost the entire patch of cleared stone was now covered in moss again, newly grown. Was this some cruel fae trickery?

Tears prickled my eyes. I was exhausted. I'd been working for hours. And now, it had all come undone. Was this part of the punishment?

If Gallis noticed my failure, he didn't say anything. He took the hoe and turned to walk back into the shadows.

I dragged myself back to the North Tower. The climb up the stairs seemed insurmountable after that backbreaking labor. I thought furiously of Selene and her smirk, and Lucien and his coldness. I loathed all of them. The whole cruel, snobby, elitist bunch.

When I reached my room, Lyrica and Hannah weren't there. I went straight to the tub and let the water fill around me as I lay in a fetal position and sobbed.

I'd only been here for a few days, and already I wanted to give up.

The hot water filled the tub to the brim, and I turned it off and let my throbbing muscles soak as the water turned muddy around me.

Finally, after the mud had settled to the bottom and the water turned cold, I grabbed a towel and climbed out.

When I returned to the main room, something lying on the ground caught my eye.

A letter.

I snatched it up and saw my name written in Grandmother Azalea's handwriting. I tore open the envelope and hungrily devoured the words.

My mom and grandmother were fine. They missed me. They were still trying to determine why I was in danger and who'd tried to hurt me. The green beans in the backyard were ripening. A stray kitten had shown up on the front porch and refused to leave, so they'd adopted it.

I read the letter over and over, soaking in every line. I let myself cry a little, and then I folded the letter, put it under my pillow, and got dressed.

I was going to be the best student Spellwood Academy had ever seen. I was going to make them proud. I'd hold my head high, study hard, and pry up that damned moss until my punishment was finished. And then I'd join Flameforge and Tearly would teach me to become a master at archery.

Okay, at this point I was daydreaming.

And most importantly, I wasn't going to let Lucien and his band of cruel friends see me cry.

CHAPTER TWELVE

THAT NIGHT, I dreamed half a dozen strange nightmares, all of them haunted by visions of boys with antlers in their dark hair and girls with eyes like black river stones. In the end of every dream, someone tried to strangle me in darkness, but I was saved by a hand in mine and a voice humming a strange, mournful song. The last dream went on and on, with golden-tongued fairies singing overhead as I joined Flameforge, which for some reason was made up entirely of centaurs. I looked down, and I was a centaur too. Then hands closed around my throat, and the lights went out, and I couldn't breathe. Pain filled my chest, and I struggled and fought, determined to live. Thunder crackled overhead, and I was lying on the road again, my bike a ruin of tangled metal beside me, and a doctor with bright eyes leaned over me and whispered that I was going to die if I wasn't careful.

I woke up with my pulse still pounding and adrenaline jolting through my veins. I lay still as the dream subsided, staring at the ceiling, and when morning came, I was resolute.

I was here to stay safe. I was here because someone had tried to kill me. I needed to remember that. I needed to be sensible. I would be a perfect student. I wouldn't do anything else to get me in trouble with the headmaster. I would make Grandmother Azalea and my mom proud.

But despite my resolution, the dark tang of my dreams lingered all through the morning.

~

I had six courses that semester, all of them shared with Hannah. Histories of the Folk, Basic Courtly Manners, Introduction to Small Magic, Survey of Political Histories and Genealogies (otherwise known as Genealogies), Practical Stratagems for Mortals Among the Fae (otherwise just known as Practical Stratagems), and a once-a-week evening class called Danger and Defense for Mostly Mortal Minds and Bodies. I hadn't yet attended that one.

It was a relief to have Hannah's familiar face with me as I walked into my Survey of Political Histories and Genealogies the next morning. I tried my best not to catch the eye of any angry-looking fae students this time, lest I inadvertently get myself into more trouble. I was still smarting from the injustice of my situation. I didn't want to bring more censure upon my head.

Professor Annita taught the class. She had ram-like horns sprouting from the sides of her head, and scarlet-red hair pulled back in a tight bun. Her smile was sharp as a razor.

"How many of you have heard of the seelie and unseelie courts?" she asked during one of our early lectures.

Half the class put up their hands. I wasn't sure if I should or not—I'd heard the term, but I didn't know what it meant.

Professor Annita sighed and shook her head.

"Every year," she said, "the mortal world's knowledge of the fae grows weaker. Fifty years ago, when I first began teaching this class, every single one of you would've had your hand in the air."

Fifty years ago? I was shocked. She didn't look older than thirty.

"Seelie," Professor Annita continued, "refers to the fae who draw their power from the light, sometimes seen as the more favorable to mortals, the kinder fae. Unseelie refers to the fae who draw power from the night, from the dark, who are said to be dangerous to mortals. Of the seven fae courts within the kingdom, four are considered Seelie—the spring court, summer court, autumnal court, and sun court. Three are considered Unseelie—the winter court, water court, and, of course, the dark court, which is ofttimes called the dark court."

She surveyed the room. "Most of the students at Spellwood—including almost everyone in this room—is descended from the seelie courts. We simply do not get very many students from the unseelie, for they do not often mingle their blood with mortals. While the notion that they are cruel to mortals as a whole is a fabrication of mortal imagination, it is true that the winter, water, and dark courts have less dealings with mortals. In fact, we have only one student at Spellwood from the dark court."

"Lucien," Hannah whispered to me.

She tapped a map on the wall behind her that showed the fae kingdom. The paper shimmered, the lines of the courts ebbing and flowing like a tide. "Over the years, the divisions between the courts have often flowed along these Seelie and Unseelie lines. And for understandable reasons, at times. A thousand years ago, the sun and dark court were at war, and they used their natural means of magic to poison and destroy each other."

Annita paused dramatically. "Light devours the dark. And dark seeks to extinguish the light. For centuries, the powers and alliances between the courts were divided along these lines. Light and dark. And understandably so, for the power of a sun fae can prove lethal for a night fae, and vice versa. The famed queen of the long night herself, Queen Roia, is said to have disguised herself as a mortal and poisoned King Bruthalas of the sun court with a single kiss, so great was her power."

One of the students raised his hand. Professor Annita nodded to him, and the student exclaimed, "But I'm from the spring court. My boyfriend is from the winter court. Will I poison him if I kiss him...and things?"

The professor shook her head. "No. The only danger is between descendants of the sun and dark court, and even then, the threat of death is only a concern for those with strong royal blood."

I thought of Lucien again. Maybe that was why he seemed in such a foul mood all the time. Perhaps he was in love with someone from the sun court. Could it be one of Griffin's friends? One of the triplets, maybe?

The lesson continued, but I couldn't focus. I couldn't stop thinking about Lucien.

~

"You look distracted," Tearly said at lunch, drawing me out of my thoughts as I tried to avoid looking at Lucien's handsome, troubled face bent over the book in his lap.

I lowered my voice. "I have a question."

"Yes?" she leaned forward to hear me better. "If it's about that siren who claims I kissed them in the observatory—"

"What? No. It's about, ah, the dark and sun courts."

Tearly waited for me to continue, and Lyrica and Hannah scooted closer to listen.

"If people from the dark court can't, you know, touch people from the sun court without getting poisoned," I asked, "then how does Lucien even exist?"

"It's complicated," Tearly said. "The dark and sun court stuff, I mean. They can touch some, but it's dangerous, especially depending on the level of power of the fae in question and the nature of the touching. I don't know how it works. Nobody here does. As for Lucien—I heard his mom died having him, and that the dark and sun courts both consider him a freak of nature. How he exists at all, I don't know. You'll have to ask him."

I certainly wasn't going to ask the guy who hated me how his parents had been able to have sex. The mere thought made my ears burn. "No thanks."

"How were your classes?" Tearly asked, taking a bit of her food with a mischievous look.

"Compared to the previous day, almost boring. A lot of lectures, a lot of assigned reading, a lot of maps," I sighed.

"No one does the assigned reading," Tearly said in a confidential tone.

Hannah raised an eyebrow, skeptical of this statement. "Then why assign it?"

"Oh, you know how teachers are," she said with a wave of her hand. "They live to assign things. But

89

really, no one does it. We're here mostly to keep us safely out of the way."

"What do you mean?" I asked, keeping my voice steady. I hadn't told anyone else about my need for safety within Spellwood's grounds.

"We're all somewhat mortal," Tearly said. "Think about it. Most of the elites are bastards. I mean," she clarified with a grin, "not only are they irritating jerks, but they are also illegitimate. Products of untimely affairs or doomed romances. This school was created by a few sympathetic and powerful mixed bloods so the important fae would have somewhere to send their inconvenient offspring. And at some point, I don't know when or why exactly, they decided to let in the riffraff too. The middlings. Us."

"You'd probably know why if you did the reading," Hannah pointed out.

"The point is," Tearly finished, ignoring Hannah, "we're not here to get top marks in the History of Mortal-Fae Relations. Nobody really cares. The mortal realm doesn't know about this school and they won't be requesting transcripts—and if they do, you can make up whatever you like—and the fae certainly don't give a puff about grades. They barely educate their own children as it is. They just let them run around the forest hunting unicorns and catching starflies."

"Is that true?" I asked, astonished. I couldn't always tell with Tearly.

"It's sort of true," Tearly said.

Lyrica shrugged in agreement. "Fae children don't spend much time with books or teachers."

"Then why have classes and grades at all?" I asked.

"Well, that's the mortal realm influence," Tearly said. "And lots of us grew up in the mortal realm, or at least spent our summers there. It isn't so foreign to us. And it is a bit of a challenge—and learning experience—for the more fae among us. Thus, true harmony. Or something like that."

"Well," Hannah said, "if nobody gives ah, er, a fig about the reading assignments, then what do they do instead?"

"You have to show up to classes, and you can't act too cavalier about it, or you'll be put on probation," Tearly explained. "And there's riding, and sword fighting, and archery."

"Sword fighting?" Lyrica said. "Archery? Who does those things?"

"I do," Tearly said, a proud note in her voice. "I'm the best shot at Spellwood, and in my court too, except for my brother—" She broke off, looking pained, and I wondered what about the mention of her brother caused her heartache. I remembered Isadora's cruel remark the first day we'd met, and how Tearly's face had stiffened with hurt and rage.

I wasn't going to ask.

"Well, is there anything for those of us who aren't amazing archers?" Lyrica asked.

"Most students spend a great deal of time with their societies," Tearly said. "Or they hang out with friends. Playing games on the lawns, going on adventures in the west woods, asking questions at the wondering well—"

"Wondering well?" I interrupted, intrigued. "Do you mean wishing well?"

"No," Tearly said. "The wondering well answers questions. It doesn't grant wishes."

A well that answered questions... I could think of a few uses for that.

"I've heard about the wondering well," Lyrica said proudly. "Is it as magical as people say? Does it really work? I want to ask it about Alcorn."

Tearly looked thoughtful. "I've got a break between classes soon. We could go together, all of us."

"And I can skip mine," Lyrica said. "It's just Minor Potions. The professor never takes roll. He won't even notice I've gone."

Hannah and I were more reluctant.

"I'm already in trouble," I said. "I don't want to cut class and end up with more detention."

"You all might be used to skipping school," Hannah said, "but I never missed a day in the mortal world. I got awards for it every year."

But as luck would have it, our next class ended up being cancelled due to a stink bomb released in the classroom, and we were left to wander on the great lawn in unexpected freedom.

Lyrica and Tearly found us soon after.

"We heard about your good fortune," Tearly said with a grin. "Shall we check out the wondering well, then?"

~

The wondering well was located at the end of Westerly, behind a crumbling, moss-covered stone wall and a brace of trees with silver bark. The well was a bit unremarkable—just a circle of stacked stone, with a dilapidated roof smothered in vines and brambles.

We peered over the edge at the dark water far below. Our faces and a patch of sky reflected back at us, rippling and distorted.

"How does it work?" Lyrica asked, her voice echoing off the walls of the well.

"I read that you have to drop in a stone and ask a question," Hannah said.

"Stones never work," Tearly said. "Everyone's thrown in a stone. The well doesn't want stones. You have to put in something unique, or something that matters to you. A pencil. A journal. A piece of jewelry."

Lyrica stared at her hand a moment, then pulled off her ring and held it out.

"Am I meant to marry Alcorn?" she asked, and let the ring drop with a plunk into the dark waters.

We waited, but no sound came from the well.

"Is it supposed to answer right away?" Hannah asked after a pause.

Lyrica leaned over the side and scowled. "I should bloody hope so. I just threw in my ring!"

"Hello?" I called, peering into the well, my locket dangling from around my neck and my hair falling into my eyes as I stared down into the musty darkness. "Can you answer our question, please?"

A ripple of wind brushed over me, raising the hairs on the back of my neck, and I felt the prickle of something like words forming at the edge of my hearing.

Sometimes love is fast as fire, sometimes love is fraught with ire, sometimes love is doomed at birth, and sometimes love has unexpected worth.

Tearly gripped the side of the well. "You got an answer!" she whispered in hushed excitement. "I've never heard it give an answer before!"

"But what does it mean?" Hannah asked. "How can it be an answer if you don't know what it even meant?"

Lyrica appeared unperturbed by the perplexing nature of the answer. She clutched her hands to her chest, her eyes brimming.

Another brush of wind teased the edges of my hair. I stared deep into the well, my own question on my lips as I leaned far over the ledge, getting as close to the water as I dared.

"Who is trying to kill me?" I whispered to the water below, keeping my voice too low for the others to hear.

But I didn't have any coins. Anything to throw in. With a sigh, I reached behind me to pull myself up, but the rock my hand landed on came loose. I pitched forward with a cry, and Tearly grabbed my wrist.

My locket caught on the lip of the well as I scrambled up again. The chain snapped, and the locket tumbled into the dark water as I cried out in horror.

Lyrica and Hannah rushed forward to haul me down from the well.

"My locket!" I yelped.

But the locket was gone.

And the otherworldly whisper came again, sweeping over me like a shiver.

Sometimes foes are mistaken for friends, and friends mistaken for foes. Sometimes danger is found in delight, and delight in dark of night.

I slammed my palm against the edge of the well as tears sprang into my eyes. "That isn't an answer!"

I'd lost my locket, the only tangible reminder of my home, for that stupid, incomprehensible riddle?

CHAPTER THIRTEEN

"I'M SORRY, KYRA," Tearly said in an effort to comfort me at dinner over the loss of my locket. She had a frazzled look about her, as if she wasn't used to her jaunts of fancy going so awry, and she wasn't sure quite how to fix it. "I'm sorry you lost it. Truly I am."

Lyrica added, "But on the bright side, I heard that once a girl caught her sleeve on the side, fell into the well, and drowned."

"How is that the bright side?" Tearly demanded.

Lyrica's eyes widened. "I just meant, she isn't dead. You grabbed her arm and saved her from falling."

I sighed. "You're right. Thank you, Tearly. Truly."

Hannah said, "You can get another locket, can't you? Maybe one of the other students will trade you in exchange for one of your mortal things."

I rubbed my forehead. The words from the stupid well kept running through my mind. It wasn't just about the locket, but the dreams I'd had the night before, and that perplexing riddle.

Sometimes foes are mistaken for friends, and friends mistaken for foes.

Perhaps the person threatening my life didn't seem so threatening from the outside? Were they someone my family believed they could trust? I thought about how my uncle had come to kill me as a baby and shivered.

Was it my family who was trying to kill me?

Sometimes danger is found in delight, and delight in dark of night.

95

Was that supposed to mean I was in danger at night?

"Let's talk about something else," Tearly suggested after another look at my face. "No more stories about drowned girls. There's lots of other, more exciting things to talk about, like the war, for instance."

"The war?" Hannah said in alarm. "What war? That wasn't mentioned in orientation!"

Tearly grinned. "We haven't talked about it yet, have we? It starts afresh in the fall every year. They don't say anything at orientation because the teachers stay out of it, you see. It's strictly student-led. And secret."

"What is the war about?" Hannah asked.

"Oh, different things every year," Tearly said. "Last year, someone pushed a fourth year into the lake at the edge of the west woods. The year before that, someone stole someone else's journal."

"People go to war over these things?" I asked, feeling somewhat alarmed.

"Oh, it's just an excuse," Tearly said. "Then, we strategize. Hold meetings. Make alliances. Of course, they're all the same—Dewdrop and Toadcurdle, Stormtongue and Flameforge, Basilisk and Briar. Except on the years when Flameforge wants to be loner heroes, and then Stormtongue sides with Dewdrop and Toadcurdle. There was one year they joined forces with Briar, but... well. It didn't end well for them, so they vowed never again. Not that Stormtongue does much, usually—they're more interested in putting on plays and debating useless topics like the mermaid question."

I hesitated. "And the teachers don't know?"

"What is the mermaid question?" Lyrica asked.

"Oh, the teachers know," Tearly said. "Lots of them were students here once. But they look the other way as a professional courtesy, so to speak. I've heard them say it builds tenacity and fosters leadership skills among us. Or some nonsense like that. Anyway, as long as we aren't breaking any of the rules, they don't seem to care."

"The mermaid question is an oft-cited argument among intellectual fae," Hannah said in answer to my second question. "In the advent of a great battle between sea and land, do the mermaids owe their allegiance to the fish, or the humans?"

"What's the answer?" I asked.

"There isn't one. It's just something people like to debate," Hannah explained. "The answer you choose—and why—reveals your reasoning style and perspective on the world."

"Typical Stormtongue," Tearly added with an eyeroll. "They don't want to fight in a war. They just want to spend all their free time debating about a hypothetical one." But she sounded a little wistful, like she would have enjoyed being a part of the irony.

"Who usually wins the war?" I asked.

"Oh, Basilisk and Briar, usually." Tearly made a face. "They both cheat egregiously, the bastards, and being elites, most of them know how to skulk and backstab and bribe the right people. Flameforge has its honest triumphs, however. Dewdrop and Toadcurdle almost never do."

Lyrica looked over her shoulder like someone might be lurking behind her to drag her away by her hair. "But... we don't even have societies yet. What happens to us?"

"Oh, the war doesn't start until after the Summertide celebration," Tearly said. "You'll have pledged before then."

I wanted to ask more questions, like what exactly was Summertide, and how did we celebrate it?

But then, a chime rang, and dinner was over. I reluctantly left my friends for the second round of my punishment, and the spoiled prince Lucien.

I was not looking forward to this.

CHAPTER FOURTEEN

ONCE AGAIN, I arrived at the Cistern before Lucien. Dutifully, I accepted the offered hoe and shovel from Gallis and waged war upon the stubborn moss.

The patch I stood upon was dotted with white mushrooms, some of them smaller than my pinkie finger, others large enough to serve as a table for dolls.

I paused amid my struggle to pry up the clinging moss. A faint, silvery sound was coming from somewhere close by. Almost like the sound of wind chimes, if someone took the sound and stretched it out like taffy.

I looked over my shoulder for the source of the sound and saw Lucien on the other side of the Cistern, ignoring me as he bent over his shovel. The wind blew, catching the edges of his hair and blowing it over his eyes.

As if he felt the weight of my stare, he turned his head and caught me looking.

I blushed and looked away.

The silvery sound shivered in my ears and crawled into my head, and I found myself absently humming to it as I chipped away at the moss.

I glanced at Lucien and saw him gazing at me with an intense expression that made my stomach somersault.

Heat rose in my cheeks, but I was angry too. "What?" I snapped after he kept looking at me.

"Where'd you learn that song?" he asked.

"I just made it up," I said, astonishment triggering an honest answer from me.

We looked away from each other at the same time. My ears burned, and I kept myself from humming for the rest of the time, though the song in my head begged to be given voice. It itched in my throat, but I ground my teeth together and stayed silent.

I didn't see Lucien leave, but when I realized the stars had come out in the purplish night sky, he was already gone.

~

My most interesting class, called by the short and easy title Danger and Defense for Mostly Mortal Minds and Bodies, was held in the basement of the library on the third day of the week.

Our teacher was a young, handsome fae who introduced himself simply as Joras. No title of professor, nothing like that. He was barely older than a student, and he had dark hair, dark eyes, and pointed ears and teeth. Everything about him was sharp and hinted at lethal danger. Strange, shifting tattoos coiled around his arms and shoulders, images of suns and snakes doing battle.

The first day, when I arrived, a few jokes flew around the room about the incident in the other class. A few students jostled each other and teased each other about being turned into frogs.

"Students," Joras thundered. "Silence."

The class abruptly quieted.

Joras glanced down at a leather book inscribed with the names of the students in the class and then pinned his dark gaze on me. "Miss Solschild, is it?" he asked without looking away.

A shiver flitted across my skin. "Yes, sir," I said, flushing at being called out immediately. What could I have possibly done? Did I already have a reputation as a troublemaker?

"There will be no charms used in my class, is that understood?"

I hadn't performed the charm. I hadn't done anything, and meanwhile, the elites strutted around campus acting like bullies and doing whatever they wanted. Was this a class thing? Was it because I was a middling who'd caused trouble? A nobody without a daddy as a king to smooth the way for me?

The injustice of it rose like bile in my throat, but I clamped my jaw on the protest I wanted to make and nodded stiffly.

"Good," Joras said. He clasped his hands behind him and paced in front of the class. "This course is intended to teach you mostly-mortals about the dangers that could await you in the fae courts. Most of you here have barely set foot in one of the courts, and right now, you're as defenseless as changeling infants. I intend to see to it that you all become wise and careful enough to avoid fae trickery and keep your heads should you venture into the fae kingdom someday." He paused, and I was certain he was focusing his attention on me again, even though he was not looking at me. I straightened, determined not to do anything to get me sentenced to more punishment.

"What is your best defense against danger?" Joras asked.

"A sword," one student called out.

"Spells," cried another.

"Wrong. Both wrong," Joras said severely. "Your best defense is the same as that of a mouse.

101

Running away. Hiding. Playing dead. You only fight back if you must. And don't even think about trying to work a spell. You'll get yourself maimed or killed. Understood?"

We murmured assent, a few of the students looking disappointed. I think they'd been expecting a class filled with hand-to-hand combat and sword fighting. Instead, we were getting the fae version of abstinence-only sex ed.

"Let's review just a few of the dangers that you could encounter in the fae world," Joras said.

The dangers, it turned out, were many. There were flesh-eating unicorns that roamed the wilderness. Sirens that could sing their prey to sleep and then suffocate them with something called Death's Kiss. The fearsome spidrys had the body of a scorpion but the face of a man, with bulbous black eyes and a cry like a woman in danger. Memory eaters devoured mortal thoughts, with attacks causing amnesia or death, and horses called nightmares that appeared only at night and caused strange, unsettling dreams in those who slept near them. And two-headed sunsnakes, and basilisks, and winterfolk, and wrogs and drogs, and babakoors, and simmergrins, and on and on. By the end of it, I was sure I'd already forgotten half of the things that could kill me, never mind the reasons why they were deadly.

When the class was over and we were gathering our things to leave, Joras called out, "Miss Solschild, if you would see me after, please."

"I'll wait for you outside," Hannah whispered, and then she joined the rest of the students and left me alone with my teacher.

Joras waited until I'd reached him. I stood before him, my fear of getting in trouble replaced by a simmering fury at being singled out and humiliated for doing absolutely nothing. I'd been a model student. He had no reason to pick on me. No reason at all.

"Yes?" I ground out through clenched teeth.

Joras pursed his lips. "I've already heard of your exploits, Miss Solschild. I wanted to remind you that I will not tolerate such behavior in my classroom."

"You've already said that to me in front of everyone," I said, trying to keep my tone even and failing.

"Temper, temper," Joras tsked. "That's exactly the sort of thing you need to be controlling, Miss Solschild. I will be watching you closely. No spells."

"I don't know any spells," I burst out. "It was all a misunderstanding."

"Dismissed," he said simply, and ignoring my protest, he turned away.

Radiating anger, I stalked outside to meet Hannah.

"How did it go?" she asked as we walked back to our room together.

"I think we should call him Jor-Ass," I growled.

CHAPTER FIFTEEN

I DISCOVERED THAT I enjoyed most of my classes, but Joras's Dangers and Defense for Mostly Mortal Minds and Bodies was a constant thorn in my side over the next several weeks of the school year. It was useful—we learned the tricks and strategies of fae safety, like how to politely decline the invitation of a winterfellow, or how to fend off a nightmare with mint and wild fennel, about poisons and draughts, of bitterbliss water that made the drinker seek out foul and brackish water to drink, and charmwine, which made its fae drinkers drunk and its mortal and mostly mortal drinkers bound to obey fae commands.

But Joras didn't seem to like me. He was forever snapping at me to pay attention, even when others around me were whispering and I was listening carefully. When we began learning methods of self-defense, he always picked me to be the one to go first. I was knocked on my back more times than I could count as Joras conjured beasts from mud and sticks to simulate the monsters we might encounter. He shouted instructions at me that I frantically tried to implement. More often than not, I ended up covered in mud while Joras informed me flatly that I would be dead in the fae world, eaten alive by a spidrys, trampled by a drog, or roasted by a flaming simmergrin.

All that fake dying was exhausting, but I was determined not to let him break me. I didn't know why he hated me so much, but I was a good student, and slowly, I learned how to dodge and weave and occasionally go for a weak spot in whatever monster he'd concocted for me to fight.

My proudest moment came one day when Joras was being especially hard on me. He'd dredged up a monster made of mud and grass and ordered me to survive against it. We were gathered at the edge of the West Woods, in a grove surrounded by oak trees and saplings. The grass was up to my knees, and the water from a nearby spring squished beneath my shoes.

I knew Joras wanted me to hide in the tall grass and crawl through the mud, but I wasn't in the mood for that kind of humiliation today. I dropped into a crouch and felt around for a stick. I knew these golems had a weakness in their center, where the magic was concentrated. I'd been paying attention to what made them collapse, and a disruption in the place where the heart would be seemed to be the best bet.

My fingers closed over a thick, straight branch half buried in the mud. I lifted it like a spear and sprang up from the grass at the exact same second that the mud creature rose over me, its hollow mouth opened wide. I planted my feet and thrust the stick straight into the monster's chest.

The mud beast exploded. Muck and bits of grass slammed into my face and rained down on the other students. I turned to face them, my stick lifted in triumph, feeling like a warrior.

I'd done it. I'd killed the thing.

The rest of the class stared at me, their mouths hanging open in astonishment.

Joras looked furious.

"Class dismissed," he hissed. "Miss Solschild, remain behind."

I wiped the mud from my eyes and waited as the others filtered back toward the school. Hannah lingered at the edge of the trees, waiting for me, but Joras barked at her to go, and she did.

After they'd all gone, Joras strode toward me, bristling with anger.

I braced myself.

"How many times do I have to tell you the point of this class?" he thundered. "Yet you keep insisting on flaunting your powers, making yourself more of a target instead of less—"

"I survived, didn't I?" I shot back. I was tired of meekly taking his anger. It never made a difference. "I'd say I fulfilled the point of the exercise. And I'm not flaunting anything. In case you haven't noticed, I'm a middling, mostly mortal, and I don't have any powers!"

He halted an inch from me, seething like a bull. "Enough," he bellowed. "Detention. Library. In the evenings."

"I'm already on detention in the evenings!" I protested.

Seriously, what had gotten into me? I couldn't seem to keep my mouth shut.

Joras scowled harder. "Six days of stocking shelves starting after Summertide. You'll be finished with your other punishment then."

Awesome.

~

My friends commiserated with me that afternoon, but they didn't let me mope about it for long.

"Speaking of Summertide," Lyrica said, "what are you planning to wear, Kyra?"

"More importantly," Hannah added, "what are you both wearing for Society Night?"

"And why is that more important?" Lyrica wanted to know.

Hannah planted her hands on her hips. "Summertide is one celebration. The societies we join will shape our future here at Spellwood and beyond." She paused. "I want to look as fierce as possible, so Flameforge will be impressed with me."

"I was planning to wear my regular after-school clothes," I said.

They both pinned me with twin expressions of horror.

"No, no," Lyrica said. "Hannah is right. You have to make a statement. An impression. Especially if—" She stopped and turned pink.

"Especially if you look too mortal," Tearly, who was lounging on my bed, finished for her.

"It's true," Hannah said with a sigh. "We have to do something clever, Kyra, if we want to stand out among those of us with wings and tails."

"You both look beautiful," Lyrica hastened to add.

"What can we do?" I asked. "Paint our faces? Dress in costume?"

"Enchantments are allowed during holidays and on Society Day," Tearly said. "For aesthetic purposes only, of course. You can always find a few kind-hearted artisans to help with your clothes in exchange for contraband."

"Contraband?"

"You know. Mortal stuff. Candy bars, CD players, etc." Tearly shrugged. "Did you bring anything with you?"

I shook my head. "Can I have something shipped to me?"

"Sure," Tearly said. "There's a whole black market for bubble gum, for example. Or playing cards. Fae love playing cards for some reason. They're fascinated by them. They think they have power. And fae folk love to gamble."

There was so much I still had to learn, I thought.

That evening, I wrote my mom and Grandmother Azalea a letter asking them to send a few things and telling them about my first few weeks. I left out the part where I had been falsely accused of using magic on a fellow student. They had enough to worry about right now with my life being threatened and the mystery of the mark on my arm. Although the mark had faded, my memory of what the dark swirls had looked like under my skin still stuck in my mind like the aftertaste of a nightmare.

At dusk, the others had told me, a stag came to collect letters that needed to be sent, with birds perched on his antlers. The birds fluttered up to the windows to fetch the letters and brought them down to the stag, who pulled a small cart behind him.

I had never witnessed this exchange, since I'd spent most of my evenings so far in the Cistern with Lucien. I left the letter with them for the birds and the stag to collect and set off alone for my punishment, my muscles already aching at the thought of what lay before me.

The moss had completely regrown. It was as if I'd done no work at all.

Maybe I should just sit on the ground and do nothing. It was all the same, wasn't it?

But no. I was trying to prove that I wasn't some weak mortal. I wanted to show all of them—Lucien, Headmaster Windswallow, Selene, who'd gotten me into this mess in the first place—that I didn't give up. That they'd have to make room for me, because I wasn't turning around and going home.

I attacked the moss with savage cuts from the tip of the shovel. A frustrated growl slipped from my lips as I strained to wrench it free from the stone.

I didn't even see him until he reached for my hand.

Lucien.

I pulled back, startled, the shovel clutched in my hands. Up close, his eyes were like a forest in summer, all green and gold. His dark hair fell over his antlers, nearly concealing them, but the tips peeked through the waves. He looked like a young forest god.

"What?" I said, pretending indifference as I swallowed my frustration.

He matched my attitude with a tone of total disinterest. "You're doing it wrong."

Furious words rose to my lips. I struggled to contain them. Some sarcasm slipped through. "I thought you were a prince. I'm surprised you would know anything about menial labor."

His eyes sparked at my jab, as if I had struck a nerve.

"Look," he said. "Your constant failure to clear the moss is bothering me."

"Bothering you?" I demanded. "Forgive me, your highness. I didn't mean to bother you with my backbreaking punishment that isn't even my fault to begin with. If your friend hadn't framed me—"

"What friend?" he snapped. "Stop telling lies."

"Selene," I hissed. "She choked the student, not me. I don't have any powers like that. I'm a middling, remember?"

"Selene wouldn't do that," he said.

I chortled in astonishment. "You doubt the cruelty of your little elite crew? Please. You all have a nasty reputation. Sorry if I don't believe your protestations of her innocence."

"I'm not making protestations of innocence. I'm telling you the facts. Selene wouldn't do that."

"And why do you expect me to believe that?"

"Because Selene can't cast spells," he snarled. "Her father stole her magic from her as a child. He used her and abused her because of her mortal blood, just as all fae fathers do."

Oh.

I was startled into silence, into sudden remembrance of what my mom and grandmother had told me about my father's family. How my uncle had come with a sword to take me. How they'd kept me secret for fear of my relatives taking me away.

All fathers, he'd said.

He was most certainly talking about his.

My anger ebbed, replaced by sadness.

"I'm sorry—"

"Don't," Lucien said. "I don't want your pity, and neither does she. I'd rather you hated me."

"Fine," I said. "Go away, then, and leave me alone."

If he didn't want pity, I wouldn't pity him. He was an ass whether or not he had a cruel father.

Was it my imagination, or did Lucien's lip twitch in a smile?

"First, let me show you what to do so you can contribute to the night's work for once," he said, and dropped to a knee beside the moss. He plucked the mushrooms growing closest to us. "You have to uproot the mushrooms first, or the moss holds on

110

to the stone. Once the mushrooms are gone, it comes up easily. See?"

The mushrooms made musical sounds when plucked from the moss, and once unmoored from the ground, emitted soft, single notes that stretched on and on.

So, that was the music I'd been hearing.

Lucian was scraping up the moss with his bare hand now, but I forgot everything else in my wonder. I dropped to the ground beside him and picked one, holding it to my ear. The sweet, pure note was like a windchime in a waterfall.

"They play music," I breathed.

"Yes," he said, looking at me with an inscrutable expression. "The nyms write songs with them."

I picked another mushroom, a smaller one with a pointed cap, and the note it emitted was high and clear. I picked another, a squat fat one, and its note was lower, deeper, like the song of an oak with deep roots.

Something inside me tugged at this, like the memory of a memory. I arranged the mushrooms in a line, and the notes changed slightly, playing off each other, alternating.

They were singing a song now, in a wild fae kind of way.

I moved the mushrooms around so they played the song that had been stuck in my head.

Lucien was still, listening to it. One of his hands twitched, and he closed his fingers in a fist.

"Are the mushrooms... sentient?" I asked.

"No," Lucien said, and his voice was strained. "No more than any tree in the forest, anyway."

That made me throw a startled glance at the forest. I didn't really know what he meant by that.

111

I picked more mushrooms and arranged them in swirls and circles as I discovered that the patterns affected the songs too. Music bloomed around me, mournful and melodic.

Lucien stood and went back to his side of the Cistern, but I felt his attention for the rest of the hour. He was watching me like I was a puzzle he was trying to solve.

I ignored him.

If he wanted to hate me, fine. I'd hate him too. We could hate each other quite happily for the rest of my stay at Spellwood, as far as I was concerned. He'd probably gotten into that fight by insulting a poor middling student minding his own business.

When the dusk came, darkening the Cistern and making it hard to see, I was almost sorry. I gathered a few of the mushrooms to take with me.

Once again, Lucien disappeared before I even noticed it was time to leave.

~

The next night, I practically ran to the Cistern. The mushrooms I'd brought back with me hadn't survived the night, but had withered into little worm-shaped pieces as hard as driftwood and as silent as stones. I'd swept them into a drawer in disappointment that morning.

I wanted to play with the music again.

I'd already plucked and arranged two dozen mushrooms in order of their musical notes when Lucien arrived. I felt his gaze on me, though he pretended he was hard at work when I glanced his way.

Whatever.

I was working on a song. A more complicated version of the simple one that had been stuck in my head for days now. I arranged and rearranged the mushrooms, discovering that I could make mild alterations to the notes they produced if I split them in half or crumbled the tops.

The moss lay forgotten around me, but I noticed that where I'd picked mushrooms the day before, it had withered away on its own. No shovels needed.

I'd been doing all that backbreaking work for nothing.

The first half of the song was perfect. I brushed my fingers over the toadstools, my heart tugging at the tune. But the second half was giving me trouble. I couldn't quite grasp what I wanted it to be, but I knew what I'd tried so far was wrong.

I was still mentally chewing over what to do when a few notes drifted on the wind. The notes that had eluded me like a whisper just out of earshot. I lifted my head.

Lucien had arranged a few of the mushrooms on his side of the Cistern. The notes were perfect.

I forgot for a moment that we had agreed to hate each other.

"How did you do that?" I said, breathless. "It's perfect. I know it's right. I don't know how I know, I just..."

"You remember it?" he asked.

"Yes." I stared at him.

"I do too," he said. "I don't know why. I've heard that song in my nightmares for years."

Nightmares.

He turned his head away. The first stars had come out. It was time for us to leave.

Did he think I was purposefully trying to torment him?

We locked gazes.

Something in his made my stomach flip, but not in a bad way.

He looked... wistful. Intrigued, and frustrated by it. Guarded.

I wanted to say something, but before I could think of why, let alone what, he rose to his feet and disappeared up the path.

CHAPTER
SEVENTEEN

WHEN I RETURNED to my room that night, I discovered that my mom and grandmother had replied to my letter with one of their own. I read it eagerly, hungry for any word from them, aching to hug them both and tell them everything I'd seen and done so far. I missed them fiercely. I wished I could feel the warm squeeze of my mom's hands and smell Grandmother Azalea's perfume as I snuggled between them on the couch with some of her herbal tea in a mug balanced on my lap.

The letter didn't tell me much about the thing that we were all worried about—the attempt on my life and their efforts to learn more about why it'd happened—but they did tell me all the neighborhood gossip, and they included some sticks of gum, a strip of bubble wrap, and a handful of peppermints.

I read their letter over and over and wished I still had my locket. I missed them fiercely.

Before breakfast, I wrote them back, and tried to keep tears from falling on the paper. I had a thousand things I wanted to say and a thousand more that I wasn't sure if I should tell them. Should I mention the things I'd heard at the well? I could only imagine the horror my escapade might inspire in my mom, especially if she knew anything about the incident of the drowned girl.

I hesitated, then scribbled a confession about the lost necklace. That way, they wouldn't wonder why I never used it.

I left the letter unfinished, and how much to tell my mom and Grandmother Azalea plagued me all through the morning.

To make matters in my head even more tangled, after lunch, Griffin appeared and asked to walk me to the library.

I could feel Lucien's glower on us over the pages of his book. He probably hated that his half-brother found me interesting. For some petty reason, this pleased me—probably more than it should have.

I said yes.

The Spellwood library was in a round, dome-roofed building set back at the edge of the west woods, with a rectangular fountain in front that was clogged with water lilies so thickly that I couldn't see the bottom. Inside, the shelves seemed to lean toward each other like gossiping old ladies, the shelves laden with leather-bound books of history and lore, all the reading that nobody but Hannah seemed to be doing.

I wondered why Griffin wanted to take me here. He didn't seem the type to enjoy browsing through dusty piles of ancient literature.

He led me up a spiral metal staircase to the second level of the library, where a skylight in the top of the dome let in a column of sunlight. Here, the shelves were shadowed, and I saw only the occasional other student lounging at a table or in an overstuffed chair.

"This is Basilisk territory," Griffin said proudly. "We won rights to it in last year's war. The others aren't supposed to come up here, except Briar.

They're allowed." He smiled like a benevolent king granting clemency to an ally as he said it, and I looked past him and saw a female student with flame-colored hair and red eyes watching us before she turned and vanished among the rows of books.

"What if another student needs a book from this level?" I asked, glancing around.

"Nobody does the reading," he said with a roll of his eyes. "And anyway, these books are never used. They're all about the eighth court, which doesn't exist anymore. And there are librarians. They can get it."

"An eighth court? What was it called?"

But Griffin wasn't listening. He took my hand and pulled me toward a back row of shelves. The row was dark as a cave and had a pleasant, dusty smell to it that made me think of curio shops and dried rose petals. Griffin put a hand on my hip and tugged me close, and I knew what was coming. I kissed him because I was curious about kissing a fae elite, and because it felt powerful and a little bit nice. His mouth was warm like the rest of him, and he was a good kisser. I put my arms around his neck and he pressed me against one of the bookshelves. The spines bumped pleasantly against my shoulders. I closed my eyes.

We stopped when the clock rang, calling us to afternoon classes.

~

At dinner, I saw the flame-haired student sitting with Lucien and his crew.

Awesome. They had a spy.

117

~

"You ought to stay away from my brother," Lucien said later while we worked in the Cistern. I was once again clearing the moss, having found myself uncertain about playing music with Lucien around. I'd made tremendous progress now that I knew the trick to it.

"Why?" I shot back, startled that he was speaking to me and angry that he was daring to try to make such outrageous demands. "Because he's an elite and I'm just a middling?"

I thought he would deny it, but the dark fae prince said simply, "Yes."

Something inside me snapped with anger. "I don't have to listen to this. Go away."

"He's dangerous," Lucien said, turning his head away from mine. I could see his lips and chin in profile, lit by the fading sunset. "His world is dangerous. Powerful. Full of politics and trickery. It isn't like your mortal realm."

"And what do you know of my mortal realm, prince?" I said. "Do you think I know nothing of danger? Of risk? You know nothing about me. You may have had a cruel father, but I had no father at all. I grew in an place where most people had bars over their windows to keep thieves out. Where you could get robbed at gunpoint while checking your mail. I know a little bit about danger."

I saw his throat move as he swallowed. He didn't answer.

I turned back to the moss. Dozens of retorts filled my head, but I ground my teeth together to hold them in.

"Guns, yeah?" Lucien said after a pause.

118

"Yes. Guns. You know what that is?"

"I know what that is."

We worked a little more in silence.

"Did you ever go to a library?" he asked.

I glanced up in surprise. "What?"

"A library. A place with books—"

"I know what it is." I pulled a few mushrooms before answering. "The library by our house didn't have a lot of books, and people were always smashing the windows."

"Oh."

"But," I added. "There was the city library. I liked to go there after school and read on one of the couches until my mom got off work, or do school projects. I was there before—"

Before the accident.

I stopped talking.

"Before what?" Lucien asked. His voice was carefully neutral, but I knew he was curious. He had a hungry expression on his face.

"I was in an accident before I came here," I said. "I almost died."

We looked at each other. I felt strangely close to Lucien. Almost close enough to confide in him. I brushed my fingers across the place on my wrist where the mark had been, and Lucien's eyes dropped to it.

Before I could say anything, I heard something. A scraping sound like branches against a grave. The hairs on my arms prickled in alarm, and I turned and fell silent at what I saw.

Something had come out of the forest.

It was a dog. No, not a dog, a tree twisted in to a canine shape, with branches for a body and roots for legs. The head was a mass of writhing vines that

119

curled and grasped blindly forward like the reaching tentacles of an octopus, if that octopus was made of rotting wood.

It looked like something out of a nightmare.

Lucien leaped up as the creature paced toward us.

His shovel and hoe were on the ground a few yards away, out of reach. The creature was between him and them.

The creature growled, and the sound was like rotting wood breaking over stones. It didn't have eyes, but it had a mouthful of teeth. I didn't understand what it was, but I knew it was bad.

The thing growled again, and this time the pitch of the sound changed like it was about to attack.

I moved instinctively. I grabbed my shovel and hoe and stepped toward the fae prince and the creature stalking him.

"Lucien," I shouted.

He didn't turn to look at me. He kept his attention fixed on the creature. "Get out of here, Kyra," he said. "Run."

I didn't run. I moved closer. It was impossible to hold the shovel like a proper weapon with the hoe in my hands too, and Lucian wasn't looking at me, so I dropped the hoe at my feet in order to better brandish the shovel. The clattering sound rang across the Cistern, echoing over the curved stones, and the creature's attention snapped to me. The roots and bark along its back bristled. It had no eyes, but I felt its stare somehow anyway.

"Kyra!" Lucien snapped, and he sounded more frightened than angry. "Go!"

In response, I kicked the hoe in his direction. It slid across the moss-cleared stone and bumped into his leg. Lucien reached down and snatched it up as the creature decided not to bother with me. It lunged at him, and he jammed the hoe against its neck.

It wasn't enough to stop the creature.

I had to do something.

"Run!" Lucien shouted again, but I didn't listen. I stepped forward, planted my feet, and swung the shovel at the creature's neck with every ounce of strength I had.

CHAPTER EIGHTEEN

THE SHOVEL SLAMMED into the creature's chest with the full force of my rage, and the creature wilted before my eyes into a pile of sticks and roots.

Lucien dropped his hoe. He stared down at the sticks on the ground.

"What was that?" I asked, my voice shaky now that it was all over.

"A fragmyr," Lucien said, sounding as breathless as I felt. He poked the sticks with the toe of his shoe. "It's just kindling summoned by a spell, but it won't stop until it's destroyed or the person it was sent after is dead. Where did you learn to hit them like that?"

"Jor-Ass's Danger and Defense for Mostly Mortal Minds and Bodies," I said. "And what do you mean, it won't stop until the person is dead? Someone is trying to kill you?"

Lucien gazed at the trees with a distant expression in his eyes. "Probably not. It wasn't a very big fragmyr."

"Was it sent from the dark court?"

He frowned. "No. At this size, it wouldn't have been able to come from far away. It was probably created here, in the west woods."

I rubbed my arms and looked down at the creature. "Who would send something like this after you?"

"You may not have noticed," he said with a hint of sarcasm, "but I'm not well-liked here."

"You seem to have plenty of friends."

"Plenty of enemies too."

I thought of the glimpse of his battered face that I'd seen beneath his glamor in Headmaster Windswallow's office. "Was it the person you got into that fight with?"

"My brother wouldn't do this," Lucien said dismissively.

Griffin? What had he been fighting with Griffin about?

I must have appeared skeptical, for Lucien added, "He couldn't, anyway, and he wouldn't hire someone else to. If he wanted me dead, he'd want to kill me himself. And he doesn't—he wants me alive and suffering."

Lucien paused, and his expression changed. He looked as if he felt he'd said too much. He picked up one of the sticks and put it in his pocket, avoiding my eyes. "A fragmyr this small is a poor excuse for an attack. No more dangerous than a dog. Probably a prank. Someone trying to get me to cast a spell and get punished further, maybe."

"Dogs can be pretty deadly," I said. Anger was gathering in me now. A prank like this could be lethal.

"Kyra," he said, startling me. For some reason, it hadn't occurred to me that he knew what my name was. "Take a deep breath."

He actually sounded worried. I sucked in a lungful of air, and realized I'd been getting lightheaded.

"Look at me," Lucien commanded, and my eyes snapped to his, which were sparkling with green-gold fire. He lifted his hand and placed his fingers gentle on the side of my face, steadying me. A pulse of something hot shot through my veins and swept over my skin.

"More deep breaths," he said. "You're turning pale."

"I'm fine," I said, not sure it was true, not wanting to be weak, not daring to move with him touching me like this.

A wind blew across the Cistern, making Lucien's hair dance across his forehead and the tips of his antlers.

Goose bumps rose on my arms.

"I've seen fragmyrs that were taller than the North Tower," he said grimly. "It could've been worse."

"Should I tell Headmaster Windswallow?" I asked, feeling shaken. "Should I go now?"

"I'll do it," Lucien said. He lifted his head toward the horizon. "It's dusk anyway. We should go now."

We walked back to the school slowly. We didn't speak, but Lucien matched his pace with mine instead of disappearing as usual. His stance was wary, almost protective.

When we reached the gravel path that led to the North Tower, I glanced at him, wondering if he was going to say anything. Wondering at the sudden lack of animosity I felt toward him.

He looked at me, but didn't speak. The darkness felt heavy and intimate around us, and I felt warm and shivery at the same time.

Then Lucien's expression shifted. He stepped back, put his hands in his pockets, and strode without a word down the path.

Flustered and confused, I fumbled for the door to the tower.

When I reached my room on the top floor, I'd already come up with ten reasons why I was being an idiot. Of course, he didn't like me. Of course, I was imagining things.

Hannah lifted her head from a pile of open books when I came through the door.

"You look like you've seen a ghost," she said.

"A fragmyr, actually," I said wearily. "And I thought Tearly told us nobody does the reading?"

"Oh, just, well I thought I might anyway," Hannah said, and then she added, with a note of frustration in her voice, "The only advantage I have in this place is caring to know everything when nobody else does. I'm as human as they come. If I ever want to get into Flameforge, or have any advantages at all, I have to be smart. Smarter than everyone else."

I nodded. I understood how she felt.

"Wait," she said, eyes widening. "Did you say you saw a fragmyr?"

I told her what had happened in the Cistern. She listened, fingers pressed to her lips, the books lying forgotten around her.

"You could have been killed!" she gasped.

"Lucien didn't seem to think there was much danger," I said, although inside I felt nearly as shaken as she looked. I felt a flush cover my ears saying his name. My pulse thudded as I thought of his burning gaze, his ridiculously sensuous lips.

Had Hannah noticed my blush?

"You saved his life," Hannah argued. "Maybe he will be less of an ass now."

"Maybe," I managed, my stomach knotting with unexpected and undefined emotions. I busied myself changing for bed, brushing my teeth, and readying my clothes for the next day.

"Don't say anything about the fragmyr," I said to Hannah when I'd had time to mull it over. "I don't want Lyrica or Tearly to get worried about me. They're already protective enough as it is."

Truthfully, I didn't want to field more comments about Lucien. I wanted to think about this.

A knock came at the door, and then, without waiting for an answer, Tearly barreled inside.

"Have you seen—" She began, eyes on Hannah, and then she caught a glimpse of me in the bathroom. "Oh, there you are." She seemed frazzled, and relief flashed across her features at the sight of me.

"Is everything okay?" I asked in alarm.

"Oh. Yes. Everything is fine," Tearly said, clearly not fine. She dropped onto the bed beside Hannah and threw up her hands in despair. "No, it isn't. I've been drafted to Dewdrop's recruitment planning committee!"

"Is that all?" Hannah said. She picked up her book again.

"Excuse me," Tearly cried. "But this is a disaster. This means I have to go to meetings every day until Society Night. I have to help design the cupcakes, which is harder than it sounds because our committee is headed by the most indecisive fae-person you've ever—are you doing the reading?"

"Yes," Hannah said, glaring at her as if daring her to say anything else.

Tearly took the hint. She turned back to me. "What am I going to do? As the hardened rulebreaker among us, tell me—do I dare refuse? Just not show up to any of the meetings? Will I be sentenced to scrape moss from the Cistern with you and the dark prince? Will the prince of scowls strangle me? You've survived his epic glowering, but that's no guarantee that I will!"

126

"How hard is it to design some cupcakes?" I asked, deflecting from questions about Lucien. "They have frosting...?"

"Oh no," Tearly said. "These are enchanted cupcakes. Last year, they each had a tiny forest on top made of spun sugar that had been enchanted to grow and change from spring, to summer, to fall, to winter. Remember, spells are allowed for Society Night and for holidays and galas. The committee wants me to come up with the idea for this year's cupcakes, and they want it to be better than last year."

"You can do it," I said half-heartedly. I was suddenly immeasurably tired. I cast a glance toward my bed. "Do you have any ideas?"

"All I can think of is the exact same thing they did last year," she exclaimed. "I need to brainstorm."

Hannah pushed a book toward her. "What about this?" she suggested, pointing to a drawing on one of the pages of the history books. "A castle?"

Tearly bent over the picture, examining it closely. "Hmm. That's an idea. Little castles."

~

For the next few days, every time I crossed Lucien's path, he seemed to be watching me. And I was watching him. Something had shifted between us, but I wasn't sure what. Had it been the attack by the fragmyr, or his rare vulnerability afterward? Had I done something, said something that upset him?

I was flummoxed and annoyed about my emotions.

In the evenings, in the Cistern, we migrated closer together as we cleared the moss. The mushrooms sang their strange, hypnotic songs, and Lucien ignored me, but with a casual friendliness that bordered on comradery at times. The evenings were strangely soothing—I had something to focus on, no matter how much my stomach tied itself into knots beforehand—but the rest of the days were far less so.

Finally, one evening weeks after we'd been working in the Cistern together, Lucien struck up a conversation.

"Do you like books?" he asked.

I raised my head and stared at him. His face was half-turned toward me, as if he hardly cared about my answer, but I could see by the stillness of his shoulders that he was waiting for my reply.

"Yes," I said. "I like books."

Lucien smiled, a flick of his mouth and a twitch of his eyes, and then he resumed work on the moss.

"Do you know what I like to read best?" he said after another pause.

I was expecting him to say he liked horror, or perhaps political strategy. What did fae princes usually read? The idea of them reading anything seemed incomprehensible, like a sea monster enjoying mall walking.

"Romances," he said, the confession accompanied by a flicker of vulnerable shyness that was almost instantly replaced with a kind of stubborn defiance bordering on boredom.

"Romances," I repeated.

Not what I'd been expecting.

"Mortals are so honest in their love stories. So certain about their affections. *Pride and Prejudice, The Great Gatsby*—"

"*The Great Gatsby* isn't a romance," I said.

"Isn't it?" He stretched with the lazy grace of a panther. His wavy hair had grown longer and nearly hid his antlers, making him look completely human for a moment.

"They make children read it in schools."

He tilted his head thoughtfully. "Fae children don't read anything. They play in the forest and climb trees and make flowers grow."

"So, I've been told," I said.

We fell silent. I wondered if I dared ask what I wanted to.

"You read all the time. Where did you learn, if not in school as a child?"

I left the question unasked but hanging in the silence between us.

"My grandmother was mortal. She taught me. She gave me most of my books, helped me hide them so my father wouldn't burn them. She'd bring me trunks full of them when she returned from visiting the mortal realm."

"Mortals are proud when their children like to read," I said. "It's considered a sign of intelligence."

He tipped his head back. "My father says it's my mortal blood corrupting me."

The sky grew indigo as we talked, and the stars appeared one by one. Our time was up.

Instead of heading back toward the school, Lucien drifted in the direction of the forest perimeter. I paused from gathering up my tools and watched him warily.

"What are you doing?"

Lucien glanced over his shoulder at me. "I've got something I need to check." He put his hands on the mossy rim of the Cistern and hoisted himself up onto the stone lip that formed the edge between us and the forest beyond.

I drifted closer. Alarm prickled faintly in my chest.

"We aren't supposed to go into the woods alone."

Lucien pulled his legs up and rose in a half-crouch. He looked at the forest and then at me. He reached out a hand.

"Then come with me, if you're so concerned for my safety."

I stared at his outstretched fingers. "What?"

Someone had tried to kill me. I didn't think Lucien was dangerous, just spoiled, but still. Waltzing into the woods at night with only the company of a fellow student was hardly wise. Right?

Then why did I want to do it so badly?

"Or don't," Lucien said, withdrawing his hand. His gaze brushed mine before he turned away, and the touch of it sent an electric thrill through me.

"Wait!" I called out. "Aren't you concerned about running into more fragmyrs?"

He'd already disappeared into the underbrush.

Was he insane?

I grabbed the shovel and scrambled up the stone wall after him before I had time to think. I wasn't going to watch him walk alone into danger. That wasn't remotely ethical. Last time, if I hadn't been there, he'd have been attacked. Or worse. And thanks to Jor-Ass's lessons, I was getting seriously proficient in fighting fae monsters.

I plunged into the forest after Lucien.

CHAPTER NINETEEN

ENTERING THE FOREST was like stepping into another world.

All the protestations melted from my mind as I gazed around in stunned awe. Luminous purple flowers grew in thick tangles up the trunks of the trees and dripped from the branches. Fireflies danced in the shadows and thickets. The moss was as thick as carpet beneath my feet, and a faint tinkle of windchimes drifted on the breeze like a ghostly echo.

Pale, glowing moths flitted among the flowers, casting flickering, elongated shadows among the leaves and vines as they landed.

"What is this place?" I breathed.

"Not as monstrous as you thought?" Lucien said. He was watching me with a hint of satisfaction on his face, as if he'd suspected I would be enchanted and was pleased to confirm his guess.

"This is the prettiest thing I've ever seen," I whispered. "And that's saying a lot, because all of Spellwood is beautiful. But this..." I didn't want to try to summon the right words to describe it, because I just wanted to look at it. "Everything is glowing."

"It's the closest thing to my home in Spellwood," Lucien murmured. "The dark court."

I stole a glance at him. He was staring at one of the glowing moths with wistful contemplation. Then, he shook his head and started deeper into the woods.

I followed.

The moss squished beneath my shoes. The plants around me were dark green and purple, almost black, some of them speckled with glowing spots that glittered like tiny stars. Our footsteps startled a snow-white stag with faint purple stripes, and it loped away into the velvet twilight.

"Do you come here often?" I asked, tipping my head back to see the forest canopy above. The glow of the moths and the winking light of the fireflies made me feel like I'd stumbled into a starfield.

"Sometimes," Lucien said. "It *is* technically off-limits."

"Has that ever stopped you?" I challenged.

He gave me an indecipherable look.

"What's dangerous about this place?" I asked after a pause. I could feel my pulse beating fast in my ears. Part of me wanted to return to school grounds, and another part of me wanted to stay forever in this glowing paradise.

"The forests are the edge between Spellwood and the wild fae lands surrounding it. They're ungoverned by any of the courts, and sometimes rogue creatures or fae wander through." Lucien stopped to push a cluster of low-hanging branches aside so he could look at the bark of one of the trees. "Look," he said. "Someone stripped pieces away here. Bark from this type of tree is part of the fragmyr spell."

He straightened, letting the branches drop. "Some of the protection charms from the schoolgrounds still protect us from intruders here, but the farther we go, the weaker the charms get. Middlings especially tend to wander too far without realizing it."

"Has anyone ever gotten hurt?" I asked.

132

"Yes." Lucien said simply.

We reached a grove of ancient, almost petrified, trees. The leaves looked silver in the moonlight.

A large, wolf-like dog appeared from the shadows and trotted forward to lick Lucien's hand.

The dog that had been with him the first day, I realized.

Lucien pulled food from his pocket and fed the dog from his palm. He murmured something to the dog, who pricked its ears up at the sound of Lucien's voice. Lucien patted the dog's head.

"Why bring him if pets aren't allowed?" I asked.

Lucien didn't look up from stroking the dog's head. "I feared for what would happen to Flock if I left him behind. I'm not exactly a favorite at court."

Flock the dog thumped his tail and thrust his nose into Lucien's hand. I stared at them both, aghast. Someone might kill his dog if he left it behind? What nightmare did he live in?

"Surely Spellwood could make an exception for one dog, under such circumstances—"

"Well," Lucien said, giving Flock a final pat before straightening again. "He isn't a dog."

I wasn't sure what that meant, and I was dying to ask, but I kept my mouth shut.

Lucien was skittish enough. I wanted him to know that I was safe to be around, that he wouldn't be peppered with constant, intrusive questions from me.

Our walk back to the school grounds was quiet, but in a companionable way. The forest glowed and fluttered and whispered. Once or twice, a moon-bright moth brushed past my cheek, eliciting a gasp from me.

Lucien watched me experiencing the wonder of the forest with an expression I couldn't quite decipher. He seemed almost shy, as if he'd shown me something personal about himself.

When we reached the edge of the forest, I stopped to take one last look at the dark beauty around us.

"Did you like it?" he asked.

"I loved it," I breathed. "It's almost... familiar... like the memory of a dream I had years and years ago. It's like I only just realized I've been missing a place I've never been before."

"Don't come here alone," Lucien said, studying me. "It isn't safe."

"I won't."

I looked at him, and my stomach flip-flopped at the intensity in his eyes. The wind blew a tendril of my hair across my face, and he lifted his hand to brush it away. His fingers touched my skin, and a spark of heat passed between us.

Lucien stiffened. He stilled and then pulled away.

"Goodnight," he said curtly, and then he headed for the school without another word.

I stared after him, confused by his sudden coldness.

Was it something I'd done?

~

The next day, Lucien refused to look at me in the dining hall. I caught sight of him crossing the lawn between classes, and he strode past as if I wasn't there.

When I arrived at the Cistern that evening, I tried to speak to him, and he cut me off and ignored me for the rest of the night.

After that, we didn't speak again during our punishment.

CHAPTER TWENTY

ALL OF SPELLWOOD was abuzz with anticipation, because it was finally, FINALLY, time to choose our societies.

Nobody got anything done in any of our classes. The students were distracted, whispering behind their hands and passing notes up and down the rows. The teachers scolded, threatened, and finally dismissed early in relief, as was the custom.

In our room, Lyrica and Hannah nervously planned their outfits while Tearly made a brief appearance to give a panicked speech about the state of the Dewdrop decorations before vanishing down the stairs again. Lyrica was dressed in shimmering ivory and silver, with frosted color on her eyelids and lips. She had flowers in her hair and vines of honeysuckle twined around her arms and legs and waist. She looked like an expensive cosplay of a fairy bride.

Hannah was dressed in black leather leggings and a black shirt. She had gotten someone to spell tattoos of flames across her arms, and they flickered with a dull orange glow as she moved.

I was wearing the green shirt and jeans I'd brought from home, but I'd paid a fae girl two packs of gum and a candy bar to magic an intricate golden mask across the upper part of my face. The spell felt like a sunburn across my skin, tight and tingling with heat. She'd also put flickers of gold in my hair and spelled it into braids and curls that hung down my back in a beautiful cascade.

Since my six weeks of punishment had finished, I was able to stay and get ready with everyone else. Annoyingly, I was distracted by thoughts of Lucien and his confusing behavior. What had happened that caused him to suddenly and abruptly ignore me?

When the sun sank behind the trees and the sky turned indigo, we ventured downstairs and out onto the gravel path, which had been lined with flaming torches.

The whole campus felt like a carnival. Stringed lights winked in the trees. Music drifted on the wind. Students moved past in giggling groups, the first years sticking together in their nervousness.

First stop—Dewdrop.

Dewdrop's party was held on the great lawn between the main school buildings and the library. Twinkling lanterns dangled from poles between tents made of exquisite silks and velvets in a rainbow of colors. Woven rugs in purple, pink, and silver covered the grass between the tents, forming the floor of a beautiful outdoor room. Couches and floor cushions were positioned at intervals between and inside the tents, creating a space to gather, sit, and talk. On the lawn outside, society members and potential recruits were playing games of croquet and tossing hoops. Others were dancing on a dance floor ringed with fluttering ribbons and garlands of flowers. Someone was passing out glass goblets filled with lemonade.

Already, the couches were packed with prospective recruits. First-year students swarmed everywhere, drinking lemonade and allowing Dewdrop members to paint colors on their lips and eyelids.

"Where are the cupcakes?" Hannah asked. "After all the fuss about them, I feel like I should eat six."

We looked around and spotted a table in one of the tents. A six-tier cupcake holder stood on top of it, and upon that sat the much-discussed cupcakes.

"Oooh," Lyrica squealed. "They're like little cakes! Small as cups!"

That was when we realized Lyrica didn't know what cupcakes were.

Tearly intercepted us. She was resplendent in a violet and silver dress that shimmered faintly as she moved. "Friends," she cried, spreading her arms. "Welcome!"

"We're here for the cupcakes," I told her with a grin.

Tearly gestured with pride at the tent. "Go and see what I hath wrought with my creative genius. Well, what the cook's assistant who we bribed with candy canes hath wrought."

Each cupcake was topped with a castle surrounded by clouds. Light glowed from within the castle windows.

"My idea!" Hannah said, triumphant. "I inspired you! See, this is why you should do the reading."

"There's more, there's more. Take a bite and see what's inside," Tearly urged us, and we each chose one perfect confection and held it in our hands.

Up close, the castles revealed even more detail. Tiny bricks around the windows and doors, a training green vine that climbed the tallest tower, and a horse and carriage the size of my thumb nail. I could smell the sweet scent of sugar, but I was almost sorry to demolish this beautiful work of art.

Lyrica had already bitten into hers. She examined the cake portion and gasped. "Look," she called to us. "Look inside!"

The inside of the cupcake had a hollowed portion filled with gelatinous liquid to look like a lake beneath the castle. A tiny, sugar-made staircase descended to it, and a boat of sugar sat upon the lake. Lyrica broke open the sugar castle and found that it was populated with tiny sugar people dancing before a sugar fire spelled to flicker like real flame.

"Good lord, Tearly," I said. "This is a literal masterpiece."

Tearly practically glowed at my praise. "Oh, it's all right," she said with a grin. "I suppose it's fit to eat."

A student as tall as a mountain ambled up to the table, snatched a cupcake, and downed it in a single bite without so much as a glance at the design. He turned and looked at us sheepishly when he realized we'd seen him.

"Hello," he said around his mouthful of cupcake.

"Craig," Tearly said sharply, "the cupcakes are for potential recruits and Dewdrop members only."

Craig winked at her. "Girl, you know if I could join two societies, I would join yours."

"Out!" she commanded, her cheeks flushing pink. "Go back to your fellow toads."

"Who is that?" Hannah asked after the still-smiling Craig strolled away.

"Oh, nobody," Tearly said. She flicked her hair away from her face with an annoyed gesture. "Just a guy." She straightened. "So, who's joining Dewdrop?"

Lyrica finished her cupcake and carefully wiped her hands on a cloth napkin plucked from a basket nearby. "Me," she said.

"Aren't you going to see the other societies first?" Hannah asked.

Lyrica shook her head. "I know I'm going to choose Dewdrop. I'd rather just stay here, play games, and dance."

Hannah shrugged. "Suit yourself."

After we both ate another cupcake at Tearly's insistence, Hannah and I set off across the great lawn through the warm darkness toward the promise of more parties.

We passed the pond in front of the library, which had lit torches posted all around it. Two male students clad in black robes stood in front of the pond, holding staves in their hands as if guarding something. A glance between them revealed a dark, wet-looking hole the size of a small round door, with steps leading downward into darkness. The torchlight danced on them, revealing mushy footprints.

"What is that?" Hannah asked.

One of the students answered her proudly. "We spelled a room beneath the pond. You can see through it like a glass ceiling. Want to see? We've got appleblood punch and lots of mortal candy in there."

Hannah shook her head, her hair swishing. "Er, no. Thanks."

The boys looked disappointed, but undeterred.

This must be Toadcurdle's party, then. Now that I looked, I could see lights moving beneath the water of the pond independent of the torches' reflections.

The sound of heavy metal drifted faintly from the hole.

I was curious about what the underside of the pond might look like, and I was tempted by the offer of candy, but I was unwilling to venture through that wet and muddy hole to get there, and Hannah was pulling on my arm to signal she wanted to go. We hurried toward the library.

"Toadcurdle is weird," Hannah muttered.

We reached the library and stepped inside behind a string of first-year girls who were all dressed in flowing, rust-colored gowns. They had golden flowers in their hair and branches twisted artfully around their arms and necks. One glanced back at me, and her eyes were so blue they were almost white. The effect was startling and hypnotic.

As soon as the door closed behind us, I became aware of the sounds in the library.

The clink of spoons against teacups, the passionate murmurs of arguments and orations coming from all over the room... and the drumming of raindrops against the windowpanes and roof. I looked around, startled, and saw water sluicing down the rippled stain glass of the windows. Lightning flashed, and thunder growled cozily.

"Enchantment," Hannah whispered in my ear.

A Stormtongue approached us, bearing a tray of pots surrounded by small, cage-like balls on the ends of tiny chains. Tea infusers, I realized. My grandmother had some. The pots held loose-leaf tea.

"Choose your tea," he said. "Cinnamelon, for energetic debates, if you like, or perhaps chavendolix, for tranquil discussions, or a black loblolly blend for acting prowess." He indicated the pots with a sweep of his free hand.

There must have been a dozen different teas, none of which I'd heard of before. I chose one called carrablanche, for clear-headedness and confidence according to the Stormtongue with the tray, and Hannah picked a red merith blend for strength. We spooned our chosen teas into tea infusers, and the Stormtongue pointed us toward a table of steaming kettles to fill our cups.

A stage had been erected in the back of the library, and various Stormtongue members were taking turns reciting poetry or performing short skits upon it. Most of the skits were based on life at Spellwood, filled with little references and jokes that I was just beginning to grasp after a few weeks here. Between performances, members served platters of sweet bread and tea cakes. Many of the first years, however, were grouped around seasoned Stormtongue members, engaged in conversation and debates.

My tea warmed me, and a pleasant feeling worked its way through my limbs after a few minutes of drinking it. I felt grounded and part of Spellwood, as though I'd always belonged. It was a nice feeling.

"The teas seem to be lightly spelled," Hannah said after gulping hers down. "They are quite potent, aren't they? I feel like I could run a marathon. Let's go now before it fades. I need this strength to get to the Flameforge party."

Part of me wanted to linger longer, observe the plays and ask a few questions, but I let Hannah pull me toward the door.

I could always return later in the evening, I told myself, and followed my roommate into the warm night once more.

Flameforge, Hannah explained, always held their society recruitment party somewhere difficult to reach. Only those who could make it to the party were able to join the society.

This year, they'd built a treehouse of tightly woven branches high in the trees of the west woods.

We crossed the lawn again, heading for the forest. We passed a few first years sitting on the grass, looking overwhelmed and starry-eyed at the choices they faced. Ribbons were strewn about at intervals, remnants of some earlier Dewdrop frolic, and near the tree line someone had planted a single torch, which had gone out, and was sending up curls of white smoke into the night.

We followed a path into the forest lit by red-tinted lanterns nestled among the ferns. The path wound through the trees and over gnarled and grasping roots, finally taking us up a hill so steep I had to cling to rocks in the path to make it. Hannah bounded eagerly ahead, her long golden hair flashing in the lanternlight. She'd dressed perfectly for this in her dark, well-fitted clothing. Her flame tattoos glowed in the darkness.

When we reached the top of the hill, we found a dangling rope waiting for us, the end hidden far above in the dark branches of the trees. A paper fluttered in the wind, tied to the rope with twine, with a single word inscribed upon it.

Swing, it read.

CHAPTER TWENTY-ONE

HANNAH WENT FIRST, fearless as she held on to the rope and plunged forward into the darkness. I heard her whoop with surprise, and then the rope came back empty.

I grabbed the rope, held on tight, and leaped. I hurtled through darkness, over the sound of rushing water, and crashed into a net on the other side. I grabbed for the net, letting go of the rope, and then Hannah's hands reached for me, and she helped me climb onto solid ground.

"Look," she whispered, pointing up.

Above us was the treehouse, or, more accurately, tree village. Woven platforms connected via arching bridges and tunnels of tightly bound branches, like strange and beautiful giant birds' nests. Faintly, I could hear music and laughter coming from above.

"How do we get up?" I asked. The trees were thick and had no low-lying branches to use for climbing. There was no ladder, no climbing rope, nothing.

Hannah flashed me a grin. "Well, that's the challenge, isn't it?"

"I thought the hill and the rope were the challenge," I said, but Hannah was already striding for the tree trunks as if she knew exactly what to do.

I followed.

Hannah ran her hands along the trunk as if checking for a secret ladder. Finding nothing, she stepped back and squinted at the higher parts of the trunk in the near-darkness. Then, she grabbed a lantern and made another round, examining the base of each tree carefully.

"What should I be looking for?" I asked, moving to one of the tree trunks.

"Handholds. A secret button or lever. Anything that looks like it might help us," Hannah said. She crouched down and craned her neck to see into a hole between two of the roots, then hesitantly poked her fingers inside.

I joined her in looking around the roots of the trees, but I drew the line and sticking my hand into dark holes that had probably been made by animals with sharp teeth. I ran my fingers over the scabby bark of the roots, pausing at one.

"There's a keyhole here," I said. "Look."

Hannah looked. "Then we're looking for a key," she whispered excitedly.

Another minute, and she'd found it pressed into the bark of one of the trees in a groove that fit the key's shape exactly. It was a massive, heavy, golden skeleton key with etchings and filigree on the handle.

Hannah inserted the key into the lock and twisted. A popping sound came from above, and one of the trees twisted and split in half as if it were a mechanical toy unfurling for our inspection. Handholds appeared.

"No staircase?" I said, frowning at the prospect of climbing so high with nothing but those slender nubs to support my weight. "Not even a ladder?"

Hannah bent down to put some dirt on her hands, dusting them together. "Have you ever gone rock climbing?"

145

"Not without a safety harness. Is there a spell to catch us if we fall?"

"Maybe," Hannah said. She took a deep breath and started climbing.

I looked at the tree village far above us.

I was at this school to stay safe, not flirt with more danger.

But I wanted to see what Flameforge had designed.

"Put dust on your hands—it'll keep them from slipping," Hannah called down to me, and I did as she suggested.

A rope hit me in the head as I was beginning my climb. I peered up and saw Hannah's face at the top.

"Found a rope!" she called with a note of triumph in her voice. "It's up here for the slowpokes."

I tied the rope around my waist and climbed after her, perfectly happy to be labeled a slowpoke in the name of safety.

Hands were waiting for me at the top. Flameforge members hoisted me the last few inches and helped me pull myself onto the woven floor of the treehouse.

"Welcome," one of the members, a girl with hair the color of a sunset, said gravely. "Good work finding us. You are the tenth to make it."

I got to my feet and brushed off my hands. My stomach was jumping from the climb, but I felt a little exhilarated too. "Is that a good number?"

The girl tipped her head to the side with a sly smile and didn't answer. A glance at Hannah's shining face told me that it was.

We crossed one of the arching woven bridges and joined the main party, where Flameforge members and the other eight hopefuls were drinking chilled cider and eating savory mortal snacks like chips and popcorn. I was amused at the sight of potato chips piled in ornate wooden bowls that looked like they ought to be holding dragon's eggs or something similarly epic and strange.

The others cheered for us, chanting our numbers and congratulating Hannah for climbing without the rope. Then, after we'd gorged ourselves on chips and cider, we explored the rest of the tree village, which was crisscrossed with rope bridges and clever swinging platforms and other interesting physical challenges.

"We'll meet here for the rest of the year," one of the members, a boy with hair spelled to look like a flame, explained. "We build a new member house every year for the society recruitment night, and then we use it after until the next year. Members only after tonight, of course."

"Is it safe to be out in the forest like this?" I asked, thinking of Tearly's warning the first day I'd met her. Never go in the west woods alone. Or was it the south woods?

"Flameforge isn't safe," he answered. "But it is valiant and strong."

I had a feeling Flameforge wasn't my society. I thought of the nice teas at Stormtongue and the cupcakes of Dewdrop. Perhaps I ought to take a wander through Toadcurdle's muddle tunnel just in case my people were there.

Whoops of delight sounded behind us, and I turned and saw that another batch of students had made it to the treehouse. They slapped each other on the backs in celebration and ran across the bridge to join the main party.

"Where do I sign up?" Hannah was asking the boy.

He pointed across the series of ropes and swinging wooden obstacles. "If you can cross the course, the paper and pen are at the end."

Hannah straightened her shoulders. "I'm ready." She looked at me. "Kyra?"

"I think I'm going to go back to the other society parties and take another look," I said.

Hannah nodded. "I'm going to stay."

"How do I get down?" I asked the boy. I had to shout to be heard over the excited squeals of the two flushed and sweating first-year girls who'd just reached the top of the tree and crawled over the side. "Do I climb back down the way I came?"

He waved a hand toward a tunnel-like bridge. "Follow that. It will take you where you need to go."

"I don't—"

"Follow," he said mysteriously, and turned and reentered the crowd of the party.

Hannah gave me a quick hug. "Wish me luck," she said. "Are you going to join Stormtongue or Dewdrop?"

"Haven't decided yet," I said.

"My bet's on Dewdrop!"

"And Tearly thinks Stormtongue," I replied. "We shall see."

She hugged me goodbye again—she seemed extra affectionate in the wake of her success in getting to Flameforge—and then I crossed the tunnel bridge alone. The sounds of the party grew fainter, and I was alone with the flickering lanterns and the quiet of the dark forest. I reached what appeared to be a carved wooden slide. It curled around the tree like a petrified, prehensile tongue, disappearing into the shadows below.

My stomach clenched, but I took a deep breath, sat down, and pushed myself forward.

I hurtled through the darkness, whooshing past trees as the slide went on and on. I thought it would curve downward once and end at the ground, but it was like a rollercoaster, twisting around thickets and dipping into valleys. I tried not to scream, but I couldn't help but let out one sharp cry of startled surprise as I plunged down the final and steepest drop at the end. I landed in the dirt, surrounded by evergreens, in complete darkness.

I stood and brushed the dirt from my legs. In the distance, lights glowed. Music from the other parties drifted toward me.

I wasn't far from the school.

Just as I was about to set off toward Dewdrop, I heard the ominous crunch of footsteps in the underbrush, and panic clutched at my throat.

What exactly had Tearly said about the north woods, or east woods, or was it the south woods? Which woods was I in?

My imagination conjured up a vision of a fragmyr.

I've seen fragmyrs that were taller than the North Tower, Lucien had said.

"Who's there?" I demanded, grabbing a stick from the ground in front of me.

"Kyra?" a voice came in answer. "Is that you?"

Griffin?

I pushed through the branches and saw him standing on a path with two other students behind him, all of them carrying casks on their shoulders. Griffin gleamed faintly in the moonlight as if his skin were lit from within.

"What are you doing alone in the west woods?" Griffin asked, a note of amusement in his voice. "Didn't anyone tell you that's a bad idea?"

"I just came from Flameforge," I said, gesturing behind me at the slide that was now obscured from sight by the evergreens. "I'm at the edge of the woods, really. It hardly counts."

Never mind the fact that my heart was thudding fast as a drummer's solo.

"You," Griffin said fondly, "are a brave thing, aren't you? Is that who you've joined, then? Flameforge?"

Was that humor in his voice, or derision?

"No," I said. "I haven't decided yet."

"Well, come with us," Griffin said. "We're making a delivery to Briar, our sister society."

"I..." I didn't have a good excuse, but the thought of crashing the Briar society party filled me with equal parts terror and delight. Well, perhaps slightly more terror than delight. "I thought you have to be invited to a Briar party."

"And I'm inviting you," he said, as if I were being idiotic. "Come on, Kyra." He reached out his free hand for mine.

I thought of our kiss in the library. Then, I thought of what Lucien had said. *Stay away from my brother. He's dangerous.*

Lucien had been ignoring me since our punishment was finished. I was mad at Lucien.

I took Griffin's hand.

CHAPTER TWENTY-TWO

THE BRIAR SOCIETY party was held in the old greenhouse on the outskirts of the school grounds, which was supposedly haunted. Candles lined the winding paths through the overgrown greenery inside, and chandeliers hung from the glass ceiling above. Statues were positioned at intervals, depicting, according to Griffin, past members of Briar who'd gone on to become fairy queens and powerful ladies. Somehow, the whole space was spelled so that rose petals drifted from the ceiling like rain the entire time, swirling and falling like pink, fragrant raindrops. Servers dressed in white and powdered and painted to look like the statues moved among the partygoers, carrying platters with the fanciest fairy food I'd ever seen before—rolled up mint leaves stuffed with nuts and meat, cheeses, and shots of some liquid that flamed on the top.

The greenhouse was somehow huge and intimate at the same time. The plants looked as if they'd been allowed to grow wild for some time, and vines and flowers crowded close to the paths and made leafy green tunnels where their stalks met overhead. The rose petals gathered atop the leaves like a dusting of pink snow.

Griffin led me down one of the winding paths toward the center of the greenhouse, where the main party was in full swing. The Briar members and their invited hopefuls were dressed in ballgowns that flashed and glittered. They wore masks that covered only their eyes and nose. Music filled the air, a hypnotic fae music that made my feet itch to dance, and my eyes feel heavy and sleepy.

Griffin set down the cask and opened it. Servers rushed to bring goblets for him to fill. The liquid inside was golden and thick, almost syrupy. It drizzled into the goblets, glittering in the light of the candles. It smelled like apples and sunshine, and my tongue felt dry with thirst just looking at it.

"Kyra?"

I turned and saw two of the triplets who were friends with Griffin. Sylla and Nylla, I was pretty sure, because Marit had a beauty mark on her upper lip.

The fae girls stared at me, clearly astonished at my presence. They were both dressed in pale dresses that looked like mist from a waterfall that had been enchanted to hold the shape of a gown. Delicate necklaces as fragile-looking as water droplets glimmered at their throats. They looked like water nymphs that had just climbed from some rushing stream.

"Hi," I said, feeling woefully underdressed in my jeans, but determined to be unapologetic about it. "Nice party, isn't it?"

One of the triplets raised an eyebrow. "Who invited you, Kyra?"

"I did," Griffin said, appearing at my elbow and dropped an arm over my shoulder possessively. "She's with me."

The girls frowned, but they didn't scold him.

Someone called his name, a student with curling horns protruding from their forehead, and Griffin moved away to speak to them, leaving me alone with the two fae girls.

They studied me like I was an insect that had wandered too close to their shoe.

"You're a bit underdressed," one said.

"It's edgy," the other said. "I rather like it. A middle finger to propriety and politeness."

It was my turn to frown. Their thinly veiled animosity was fast replacing my uncertainty with anger. "Aren't you supposed to be nice when talking to potential recruitments?"

"Oh, yes, of course. Why don't you join Briar? I'm sure you'd fit in perfectly here," one of them said with obvious sarcasm.

I felt the sting of her disdain like a slap, and I didn't answer.

"Sylla," Nylla murmured reprovingly as she offered me a small smile of apology. "What she means to say is, I don't know that Briar is the best fit for a middling student. We don't want you to have a bad time at the school. One's society is so important for fitting in well and having a good experience."

I rubbed a hand across my forehead, wondering where Griffin had gone and if I wanted to wait for him or if I wanted to simply turn and walk away from this mess.

"Headache?" Nylla reached for one of the goblets and pressed it into my hand. "Drink this; it'll help."

Thinking of the Stormtongue tea I'd had earlier, I took a sip. Maybe it was enchanted to make the one who drank it feel good. I could certainly use a bit of that.

The liquid was like thin honey as it fell onto my tongue. Whatever it was, the drink was delicious, like the scent of strawberries mingled with the joy of a warm summer evening and the relief of a cold drink on a hot day.

I swallowed the rest in a gulp and stared into the bottom of the goblet, wanting more. The air smelled like a thousand crushed roses, but not in an overwhelming way. The scent was perfect in its intensity.

"There," Nylla said. "You'll feel better in a minute, just wait."

I set down the goblet and glanced around again for Griffin. My gaze slid over the garlands of flowers, the flickering candles, the floating rose petals. Everything seemed to have an extra glitter to it now, and I wished Lyrica and Hannah were here with me to see this. It might be snobby Briar, but it was still beautiful.

"Want to dance?" Nylla—or was it Sylla? —asked. I couldn't remember which was which now. Their expressions looked identical.

I found myself nodding. The music was beautiful.

"You need a different dress," Sylla—or was it Nylla? —said. She reached into an unseen pocket and pulled out a vial of glistening paste. She dipped one finger into it and brushed the stuff across my collarbone and over the shoulders of my shirt before I could say anything.

"There," she said, replacing the cap on the vial and putting it away.

I looked down.

My shirt and jeans had transformed into a dark green gown with a plunging neckline. The fabric hugged my hips and flared out, mermaid-style, around my legs. Golden roses coiled up my bare arms and around my neck.

"Oh," I said, touching one of the golden roses with my finger. "How'd you do that?"

"Enchantment," Sylla or Nylla said with a flick of a smug grin. "Come on, mortal girl. Let's see how you dance."

The main party area was surrounded by more yellowed candles and dripping with garlands of roses that hung from the ceiling, forming the suggestion of a tent. In the center, people danced— elegant, heartbreaking fae dances that made my mortal-raised eyes well with sudden tears at the beauty of it. Which was rather unlike me. The dress swished around my legs, light as air, and the blood in my veins felt like fire and sunshine.

Nylla and Sylla joined the dance, beckoning to me. But then Griffin was at my side again, his arm sliding around my waist protectively. He stared down at my dress.

"You changed," he said.

"Nylla did it. Or Sylla." I was grinning a little foolishly. I felt giddy and strange.

"Did you drink anything?" he asked, his eyebrows lifting. "You seem... relaxed."

"I had some of the drink in that casket," I told him. My eyes were still on the dancers. My feet itched to join them. The music had slipped into my brain like a fever, and I was helpless against its call.

Griffin didn't take his hand away from my waist, however, and so I stayed beside him. He wasn't exactly holding me back, but it was enough to restrain me.

"Let's get out of here," he said.

"And go where?" One of the dancers twirled so beautifully that I couldn't help but giggle in delight.

"My party," Griffin said. He steered me toward one of the paths, his arm still around my waist. "Come on, Kyra."

I didn't mind the way he slightly mispronounced my name. In fact, it made me laugh.

"What's so funny?" Griffin asked, smiling down at me. His eyes gleamed golden as if faintly lit from within.

"You," I replied. It was a stupid reply, I knew, but I couldn't seem to find the need to care. His arm was warm on my waist. I felt safe and happy.

"How much did you drink?" he asked as we reached the doors of the greenhouse and stepped into the warm summer air.

"A goblet full." Some small place in the corner of my mind wondered if that was too much, and it thought about raising protest, but the rest of my happy brain squelched its concerns. It was a beautiful night. I was with Griffin, who I hadn't been sure about before, but now I felt quite comfortable and happy with his arm around me.

We followed a path lit by moonlight, past the silent school buildings, past the tower that held Headmaster Windswallow's office. I could see lights gleaming in her windows. She must be awake, perhaps keeping watch over the society goings-on.

"Where are we going?" I thought to ask after some duration.

"The Basilisk party," Griffin answered.

My stomach did a flip despite my euphoria. "I don't think I'm invited," I said a little too loudly.

"You're with me," Griffin assured me. "You are my guest."

The Basilisk party was held at the crypt, which shone ominously in the pale moonlight, surrounded

156

by a tall wrought-iron fence that groaned as Griffin pushed it open. We climbed the steps, me stumbling once, and walked down a hall lined with crumbling stone columns until we reached the entrance.

"What is this place?" I muttered, looking around me. "It's creepy."

"The crypt has been here as long as the labyrinth and the other original buildings," Griffin said as we approached the door. "Some say its haunted, but you'll be safe with me, Kyra."

The door swung open as we reached it, held by a student with downcast eyes and no shirt. He wore a golden collar around his neck.

"What...?" I said, turning toward the student.

"Ignore him," Griffin said. "He's being initiated. Everyone who was invited into Basilisk is here, and they are serving us tonight. On society night, we party among ourselves. No need to impress any new students." He laughed.

The inside of the crypt was bigger than I'd expected. Stone walls stretched upward to a vaulted ceiling. Statues and stone coffins lined the walls, and doorways led into dark, shadowed corridors that I assumed held more burial places.

Basilisk had made a half-hearted effort with carpets and candelabras to light the gloomy space. A few of the members were sprawled on stone caskets as if they were couches, joined by some Briar members in their fancy dresses. Everyone was drinking from goblets. The elected new members scurried around with platters piled high with food and drink.

No dancing, no music, no impressive or creative displays of enchantment. Just a bunch of elite snobs drinking and lounging like drunk lions.

I was less than impressed. Even in my euphoric fog, I recognized that they must think themselves above the earnestness and creativity of the other houses. They probably though such cool detachment made them refined and sophisticated, but it merely made them dull.

"Is this it?" I was saying when my eyes strayed across the room and collided with a familiar pair of green-gold ones.

My stomach sunk to my knees, and a flush rose along my cheeks.

Lucien.

He looked back down at the book in his hands immediately. I stood reeling, some of my good feelings replaced by a spinning confusion, a kind of hunger. Part of me wanted to turn around and walk right out the door, and another part of me wanted to go over to him and demand that he explain himself and his capricious, maddening moods. We'd almost been friends. At least, I thought we had. And then he'd turned cold toward me.

He'd hurt me.

The most sensible part of me whispered that I ought to ignore him. I listened to that part and focused all my attention on Griffin's face. Well, most of my attention.

I couldn't fully wrest it from Lucien, not matter how much I tried.

"Are you bored?" Griffin was saying with amusement. "Not enough fae glitter for your mortal eyes?"

"Perhaps we should play a game," someone suggested. I turned and saw that Sylla and Nylla had arrived, joined now by their third sister, Marit, who was dressed in a dress of gold that glimmered with the same shimmer as Griffin's eyes. She gave me a poisonous look. She was the one who'd suggested the game.

Griffin lifted his brows and smiled indulgently. "What game?"

"Charades," she said, taking a sip from the goblet in her hand. "Girls against boys."

Some of the others were watching us, their eyes bright with sudden interest. Like sharks that scented blood in the water, they could probably feel the dislike radiating from Marit in my direction.

I didn't remember her being like this toward me before. Had I done something to anger her?

"I'll go first," Sylla declared.

"No," Marit said. "Kyra goes first."

The liquid euphoria still swam in my veins, bolstering me. I raised my chin. "Fine," I said.

Marit leaned close. Her lips almost brushed my cheek. "Your word is monkey."

I gave her a look—monkey was not the most flattering thing to act out in front of a group of sophisticated, judgmental snobs—but I wasn't going to let her see me embarrassed. I strode to the middle of the room so everyone could see me, dropped to my hands and knees, and bravely mimicked a monkey.

Some of those watching cackled. My face flushed, but I kept going. The euphoria in my veins helped. I hardly cared what they thought. The prickles of embarrassment were overcome with a heady sensation of freedom and power.

Sylla and Nylla, as well as a few of the other Briar girls, tried to guess what I was.

"A minkwarbler!" one cried.

"A bogswallow!" another shouted, certain she'd guessed it.

Hadn't any of these girls seen a monkey before?

Perhaps not. They were the elites, after all. They were all raised in fae courts, most likely. They didn't know a computer from a toilet.

Marit smirked at me, triumphant.

Lucien was watching, and I felt his gaze on me like a brand, but I wasn't about to let her win. I redoubled my efforts, and then I remembered that a professor had talked about monkeys in one of our lectures, comparing them to a fae creature called a gobbit that had long limbs and a primate-like face that loved to eat fruit and pluck its own fleas. I switched tactics, mimicking first the gobbit and then the monkey, and playing like a mortal in between.

The strategy finally worked for one of the Briar students. "Monkey!" she cried loudly, to my relief. "It's called a monkey!"

Marit scowled.

The boys seemed disinterested in rising from their positions atop the stone coffins to participate, so one of them called over a new recruit in a gold collar and made him act out their word instead. He strutted and stumbled and acted like a drunken fool. The word, in turned out, was mortal.

Sylla was next, and Marit gave her an easy one. Sun court. Everyone guessed it right away, because Sylla mimicked the king of the court who apparently had easily distinguishable mannerisms relating to how he played with his beard.

Another poor recruit was drafted to enact what turned out to be floor-licker, apparently a fae insult. The poor fellow actually licked the floor.

When it came time for my turn again, we were winning by a single point. Marit stepped close to me, and I smelled the scent of her—mint mingled with a coppery tang like blood.

"How much charmwine did my sisters give you?" she asked with a slip of a grin chasing across her face.

Charmwine.

The forbidden drink that turned mortals into puppets and made even full-blooded fae silly and suggestable?

A cold feeling crawled through me.

This was dangerous. I hadn't sipped some mild, enchantment-doctored juice. I'd consumed a fae drug. No wonder I'd been so weepy and giggly. No wonder I'd had no inhibitions.

I tried to take a step back, but she seized my wrist. "Your word is slut," she said. "And I want you to kiss Lucien to act it out."

My stomach squeezed like a fist. My eyes shot to the dark prince, who was once again reading, one leg dangling over the side of the stone casket, his head resting against the wall. My mouth dried.

"No," I whispered, but I had a feeling that I couldn't really refuse her. I had fae blood in me, but not much. I was a middling, mostly mortal. I was practically her puppet should she insist, thanks to the charmwine. I was nearly powerless.

"Yes," she said. "Go and do it, middling. And make it passionate."

Dread sank like a stone in my belly.

Why Lucien? Why this?

I looked at Griffin and understood. She was wearing gold to match him. She was angry that I was here. She wanted to make me kiss his half-brother...

She was trying to get between us.

The command hung in the air, and I lifted my eyes to see that everyone was watching us expectantly. They hadn't heard her words, but they must have seen something in her expression. The watching faces hardened with cruel anticipation.

All but Lucien's. He was looking at me, his eyes dark with displeasure.

"Go," Marit commanded again.

The impulse from earlier tugged at me too. The desire to stalk over to Lucien and demand to know what he was thinking.

I walked across the crypt to where he and his friends were sprawled. Lucien closed his book with a snap.

"What is it?" he asked, his gaze snapped from my face to Griffin's.

I looked back and saw Griffin smirking. Confusion bloomed across my mind.

Marit was trying to make Griffin jealous, but what was Griffin thinking?

I turned back to Lucien, whose expression had turned hard. He reached out and grabbed my hand.

"Stop," he commanded, and the warmth in my veins turned to ice.

"Have you been drinking charmwine?" he asked in a harsh tone.

I didn't answer him, but the truth was clear.

"How could you be so foolish?" Lucien hissed. "Don't you know how dangerous it is? Are you that desperate for them to like you?"

"Kiss him," Marit called out in the imperious voice of one who expects to be obeyed. "Kiss him like you think he isn't a repulsive little snot."

Lucien dropped my hand. A muscle in his jaw twitched as if he were grinding his teeth together. "Stop trying to give her commands," he called back. To me, he said, "Go back to Dewdrop where your friends are," he said. "You don't belong here, Kyra."

His words hit me like a slap. The emotions in my head churned. I could hear the others laughing behind me. Griffin. The triplets.

"She didn't drink enough," Marit said in amused dismay. "She's resisting the effects."

So, it was all some scam to embarrass me? To put me in my place?

Anger rose above the shame, drowning it out. This wasn't my fault. It was their doing. I'd been too trusting, but that was usually not a bad thing.

I whirled on Griffin and Marit.

"How dare you," I snarled.

There wasn't a single trace of remorse on their beautiful faces, and I hated them for it.

"Why?" I demanded.

Their laughter quieted to giggles. Griffin gazed down at me like he didn't know who I was. "Why what, middling?"

"Why did you try to—to seduce me? You ate meals with me. You kissed me!"

Marit's smile vanished completely at that.

"And you lapped it up," Griffin said with a smirk.

"Honestly, I've had better," I responded, and strode past them for the door.

The silence outside was bracing. I stumbled down the steps for the path, my throat closing up with tears of rage.

How dare they? How dare they have such cruelty and entitlement?

The fury burned in me, strengthened by the charmwine and my resolve. I had been bullied a little in high school, but not much, and it was shocking to experience it now. Where they doing this to others?

The moon was high. The societies would be winding down soon. I needed to put aside this mess and sign up for one before I went back to my room to crawl under the covers of my bed and cry.

I knew which one I was going to pick. I'd decided.

I stormed my way to the party of my chosen society, signed my name on the ledger, and went straight back to the North Tower.

Stupid elites. Stupid Lucien. Stupid wondering well answer that wasn't true.

Although I meant to cry until I felt better, I almost immediately fell asleep.

CHAPTER TWENTY-THREE

WHEN I WOKE up, Lyrica, Hannah, and Tearly were all peering at me with expressions that ranged from curious to alarmed.

"What?" I mumbled, sitting up and then immediately lying back down with a groan.

"Are you all right?" Hannah asked. She had a glass of water in her hand, and she gave it to me. "Drink this."

"We heard about what happened," Lyrica added.

The night came back to me, first in pieces, and then all at once in a rush of horror. Griffin. Basilisk. The crypt. Lucien's coldness, and Marit's cruelty. I remembered leaving the crypt, and then nothing else.

"What did you hear?" I said, a dart of terror spearing my stomach.

"How you went to Toadcurdle after all," Hannah said. "How you stormed inside and gave them a rousing speech about not accepting the bigoted limitations of class divides or something?"

"I think you're their hero now," Lyrica added, her eyes wide. "I heard one of them say they were in love with you."

I made a scoffing sound. "I gave a speech?"

"It's true," Tearly said. "I saw you go in."

"But you didn't join Toadcurdle," Lyrica continued. "Did you?" She sounded a bit nervous, as if she wasn't entirely convinced that I hadn't.

I searched in my memories for the answer and came up empty. I had no idea. My memories from the night after leaving Basilisk were a blur of starry night sky and shadows, the taste of cupcake on my tongue and the faint scent of roses and mud.

"I don't remember," I confessed after a long, expectant pause.

They stared at me in confusion, and I heaved a sigh.

"Is there some way I can find out?"

"It's posted," Tearly said with a gasp. "In the main building. There's a list. We can go and look."

They hustled me out of bed, making impatient noises the entire five minutes it took for me to brush my teeth, make myself less gross with a sponge bath via wet washcloth, and get dressed.

"There should be charms for the equivalent of a shower," I grumbled. "And they should be allowed."

"Come on," Lyrica begged. "I can't wait another second. I bet you're in Dewdrop with me and Tearly!"

"I think probably Stormtongue," Hannah said, looking mildly disappointed like she hoped I'd joined Flameforge instead and was trying to brace herself for an alternative answer.

We hurried down the spiral staircase and into the warm, humid summer morning air. It was the weekend, and no classes, but a few students were out wandering the gardens or having picnics on the great lawn.

I noticed one or two people looking at me as we passed. Worry prickled at the back of my neck. Had they heard about how Basilisk had humiliated me?

We reached the main buildings and went inside. Our footsteps echoed. My heart pounded.

The lists were posted on the wall beside the office where I'd submitted my laugh and drop of blood the first day I'd arrived. Six scrolls were pinned to the woodwork, the names emblazoned at the top. Dewdrop's font sparkled like it was made of water glistening upon a river rock.

Tearly and Lyrica scanned the list of names.

"You're not here," Lyrica announced, disappointed. "I was certain you would be."

They moved on to Stormtongue. The list fluttered as if blown by an invisible wind.

"Not here either," Tearly said, turning to glance at me with her brows raised.

Hannah made a sound of strangled excitement. "You did choose Flameforge!"

But Lyrica, who'd moved in front of the parchment with the flaming font, shook her head. "Her name isn't here either."

Hannah covered her mouth with her hand. "Toadcurdle? Technically, anyone can join any society, but..."

"No," Tearly said. She took a step back as if in shock. She pressed her fingers to her chest. "Kyra, what have you done?"

"What?" I demanded anxiously. "What is it?" I pushed forward, looking where she was looking.

The parchment covered in brambles, with a scent of roses, and there at the bottom was my name, signed with a confident swirl.

Horror bloomed in my chest.

I'd joined Briar.

~

"How?" Tearly kept demanding as we ate lunch. "How is this possible? You have to be invited to join Briar and Basilisk, or the pen won't work on the parchment. You literally cannot put your name down unless they have given you an invitation."

"One of Griffin's triplet friends sarcastically invited me," I said, remembering. "Do you think that was enough to make it work?"

"It must've been," Hannah said. "But... why?"

"I guess I was angry," I said, trying to retrace my thoughts and coming up mostly empty. "I wanted to show them they couldn't mess with me. I must have stormed back to the Briar party and put my name down."

"Well," Tearly said. "You, ah, showed them, I guess. Congratulations. You're going to be miserable."

I picked at my food. My stomach was a mess of knots. I had no appetite. "What happens now? They can't kick me out, can they?"

"No, they can't," Tear said with a shake of her head. "They're stuck with you."

"And I can't quit?"

"Not without special permission from Headmaster Windswallow, and she isn't going to give it to you." Tearly took a bite of her sugared pork and chewed thoughtfully. "People have society regrets every year. She gives some speech at the next assembly about learning to live with our choices."

"Wonderful," I muttered.

Across the room, I saw Lucien stroll inside with his group of friends, and my face heated. His gaze caught and tangled with mine, and my stomach twisted. Lucien's expression turned dark.

I stood.

"I'm not hungry," I announced, and left to take a walk.

~

The warm air folded around me like a blanket, at first comforting, then smothering as I paced the length of the great lawn and then along the tree line. Memories of the crypt pushed through my efforts to suppress them—I kept seeing the look on Griffin's face as Marit had commanded me to kiss Lucien. Rage trembled through me—how dare they treat me, or any other middling, that way? How dare they act like I was a puppet that existed for their amusement?

I didn't notice that I'd taken the path into the forest until I was too far to see the lawn anymore.

I stopped, Tearly's warning ringing through my head.

Never go alone.

How stupid was I going to be? First joining Briar, then wandering into an enchanted and dangerous forest by myself?

I whirled to return the way I'd come and stopped as someone stepped from the shadows and blocked my path.

I breathed a sigh of relief as I saw it was only Professor Annita, who taught my Fae Court Histories and Politics class.

I smiled at her in startled relief.

"Hi," I said. "I thought you were some kind of forest monster for a second."

She didn't smile back. "Miss Solschild, is it? You shouldn't be out here alone, not even this close to the school grounds. It isn't safe."

"I know," I said, my smile fading. "I'm sorry—I was distracted. But I know it's inexcusable. I'm sorry. It won't happen again."

"It better not," she said severely, her brows drawing together.

My expression must have been stricken, for hers softened slightly.

"Come," she said. "I'll walk you back, and perhaps you can tell me what has you so distracted that you're ignoring rules now."

As we returned to the campus, I explained my dilemma with Briar. I left out the part where I'd been humiliated by Basilisk, but when Professor Annita probed, I confessed to the charmwine incident in vague terms.

"Charmwine is strictly against school rules," Annita said with a frown. "I'll have to report this to the headmaster, Kyra."

Great. Now I was going to have a reputation as the school snitch on top of whatever else they thought of me.

I figured I could worry about that later, though. One thing at a time.

Professor Annita escorted me back to the great lawn, and when we'd reached it, she said to me, "Don't worry too greatly about your choice in society. They will be your sisters now. They swear an oath of loyalty. They cannot hurt you, even if they loathe you."

"That's not the most comforting thing anyone has ever said to me," I replied with a grimace.

Professor Annita smiled faintly. "Their respect for you may come with time, and perhaps friendship. The fae are fickle folk, and Briar is populated with those of more fae blood than mortal. They will not be angry long. If anything, your surprise inclusion might win you admiration."

I hadn't thought of that. Frankly, it wasn't on my radar.

What had the wondering well said? Oh, who was I kidding? I knew those words by heart.

Sometimes foes are mistaken for friends, and friends mistaken for foes.

But that couldn't be what it meant. There was no way Lucien and Griffin's friend were ever going to like me.

CHAPTER TWENTY-FOUR

THE FIRST MEETING of the societies was the next day, at the end of the weekend. Lyrica hummed under her breath as she dressed for her meeting, which required glittery makeup and sparkles in one's hair, and Hannah stressed about what shade of black to line her eyes with to make herself look as fierce and fae as possible.

I stared at my reflection, feeling as if I had stones in my stomach.

Briar members, Tearly had informed me, always wore roses in their hair. Classic, simple.

There was supposed to be a letter, delivered by the stag and the birds. Lyrica and Hannah had both gotten a letter, with instructions on where to meet and what to wear, as well as enthusiastic greetings to all new members.

I didn't get a letter. It seemed to have mysteriously gone astray.

Luckily, Tearly knew where the Briar society house was located, and how they dressed on their first meeting day. I wouldn't wander like an idiot or show up completely lost.

Lyrica and Tearly fussed over my hair, weaving the vines and roses in among a mass of braids and curls that cascaded down my back. They used no magic, since this wasn't a special occasion that allowed it, but the result looked magical anyway.

"Thank you," I said, turning right and left to get a better view. "It looks magnificent."

"I've done well, if I do say so myself," Tearly said proudly, her hands on her hips. She had a dusting of silvery glitter along her cheekbones and curls, making her look like she'd escaped from a kindergarten craft table. She smiled at me, but her eyes were sad.

"Don't let them bully you," she said with a jut of her chin. "Show them exactly what middlings are made of."

We walked together to the bottom of the North Tower, and there we parted ways—Tearly and Lyrica heading on toward the great lawn, Hannah toward the forest, and I continued alone through the gardens.

I had the shortest walk of all of us, for the Briar society house was not far from the gardens at the foot of the tower.

The Briar house sat nestled among the trees at the edge of the rose garden like a forgotten secret, and I reached it all too soon, with barely enough time to collect my courage before I was in front of the door.

A tree wrapped half the house in clinging branches, and I realized after a moment that it was a rosebush, hundreds of years old, that had melded with the stone and plaster of the house over centuries. The house was white, with cracked columns and marble steps that led to a blue door with an arched top and a handle in the shape of a rose. Everything was cloaked in an air of hushed mystery.

The door opened beneath my hand, and I stepped across the threshold and inside.

The air smelled like rose petals and crushed violets and a hint of the kind of dusty scent of a forgotten library. It smelled like the magic of old books and summer hollows. The wooden floor creaked beneath my feet.

I heard the rush of leaves and looked up, and saw that the rose vine that had overgrown the outside of the house had somehow penetrated within it too, and clung to the ceiling, obscuring the plaster with a tangle of thick wooden branches that bit into the frame of the house and a quivering shield of leaves and drooping roses. A few petals drifted downward as I closed the door behind me.

This house didn't need magic to make it beautiful. It was breathtaking just as it was.

I followed a hall with walls papered in hunter green and gold until I came to a sitting room, painted in a deep, lush turquoise. The vine clung to this ceiling too, dangling a chandelier of flowers overhead, and there were windows, arching Palladian windows open to the wind, and little round windows of stained glass, and the room was filled with shifting, gold-green shadows that made patterns on the floor.

There, in the sitting room, perched like queens on the gilded couches and chairs, were the other Briar girls, wearing their school uniforms like queenly robes, their faces set with expressions ranging from boredom to anger.

Waiting for me in cold silence.

"There she is," one said with a scowl. Her words came out hissing. "The troublemaker herself."

The girls pinned me in place with their eyes, their gazes poisonous. I noticed immediately that none of them wore roses. They all had gold vines in their

174

hair, woven into braids or cascading free. Once again, I was the outcast. The different, strange, unwanted one. Had they done this on purpose? Had they somehow known I had the wrong information?

And I felt suddenly weary, angry, and annoyed. I missed my mom and Grandmother Azalea, and someone had tried to kill me, and their dislike of me was petty and stupid and unkind. I wish I didn't care that they all obviously hated me, but I wanted to shrink into the floor.

I wouldn't let them see that I was afraid. They couldn't kick me out—that gave me some power, at least.

Everyone was looking at me with disgust, like I was a racoon that had wandered in from the woods.

"Yes," I said in the resulting silence, since everyone seemed to be waiting for me to do or say something horrifying. My legs trembled a little, but my voice came out confident and steady. "I'm the troublemaker. My name is Kyra. Someone invited me to join Briar, and so I did, and it serves you all right. You're snobby and stuck up and you think being elite makes you better than everyone else. Well, you've got a middling in your midst now. Congratulations."

Expressions of rage flashed across a few faces.

I turned to go, and my hand was on the door when someone demanded, "Where do you think you're going?"

I turned. Selene was leaning forward with an odd gleam in her eye. A challenge, maybe?

"I'm leaving," I said. "You can't kick me out, but I don't have to sit here and have you stare at me like I'm not even speaking."

"Oh," said Isadora from her place on the couch. "You have to sit here. We aren't going to let you waltz away now. You're going to suffer." She smiled thinly, and her eyes glittered like black ice.

"Suffer," I repeated. A burst of nervousness filled my stomach.

Were they going to try to beat me up? Lock me in a closet? Unleash bees on me?

"Yes," Marit said with a somehow-elegant jerk of her head. She smirked at me. "We're putting you on the student council."

~

Turns out, every society had to send a representative to the student council. Some societies saw this as a coveted position. Basilisk and Briar, on the other hand, sentenced unlucky members from among their number to the task like prisoners going to an execution.

And now, the honor was all mine.

After declaring me student council representative, a move which they all chorused their formal agreement for, the Briar girls took an oath.

The girls formed a circle around a bowl of roses, which Selene set fire to, and then I was nudged into the circle, and everyone put out their hands. Selene drew out a dagger with a handle carved in the shape of a rose, and she pressed the tip against every new member's finger one by one, leaving beads of blood to drip on the roses below.

I expected the prick to hurt, but it was painless. I stared at the blood that quivered like a ruby on my finger while we repeated a promise to remain loyal to the members of Briar even over our respective

176

courts. The flames turned blue and silver as we repeated after Selene, and the smoke swirled around our outstretched hands and into our faces, making me cough. A cold tingle rushed across my fingers and up my arm, aching in my bones, and for a moment, the bead of blood on my finger flashed silver.

"It is done," Merit said when we were finished and had fallen silent. She looked at each new recruit one at a time, holding their gaze fiercely. She stared me down last of all as she said, "That oath is binding for life. It's in our blood now. We cannot break it. Briar is your final and utmost loyalty, and the members are your sisters. You cannot betray them to an enemy, even in service to your court."

I exhaled, wondering if this meant I would be free of their spite from now on, the student council position excluded? When they'd promised suffering, had they meant something else?

After the formal oath-taking, the newest members were given a tour of the house. Briar's society home was cozier than I expected, and smaller—a kitchen, a pantry, a cellar, the great room where we'd taken our oath, a sitting room, and then a staircase that took us to a second story with four large, gabled bedrooms. There was a second staircase leading to an attic, which apparently was haunted by wood sprites that sang at odd hours of the night.

The walls of the rooms were painted in lush purples and rich greens, magentas, and burgundies, with carved paneling covering the ceilings. The single washroom was painted robin's-egg blue, and the walls were coiled with exposed brass pipes that ended at a tub as big as a bed.

Everywhere grew the vines, the thorny strands tangled across the ceilings and occasionally creeping down the walls, biting into the plaster and dropping rose petals on the ground. The scent of roses hung heavy in the air. All the windows were open, letting in warm gusts of breeze that make the curtains flutter.

After the tour, we pricked our fingers again, this time on the thorns of the rosebush that grew through the house, and dropped the blood on the doorstep. Only members of Briar could enter, we were told.

"What about the wood sprites?" I asked. "How did they get in?"

"They were here when we took over the house," our guide, a girl named Noni, said as if I'd asked a supremely stupid question.

We ended the tour in the kitchen, where platters of sumptuous food waited for us. Honey-drizzled breads, and cream-stuffed rolls, smoked mushrooms and sugared berries, fresh fruits and vegetables gleaming with butter and sweet sauces. It all looked delicious, but somehow, mine tasted like dirt, and when I spat out a piece, I saw that it was dirt. I glared at the others, but they ignored me, eating with relish and exclaiming at the deliciousness of the food.

"Does life-long loyalty not extend to the food?" I snapped finally, after pulling a wriggling worm out of my mouth.

The Briar girls barely spared me a glance. "Oh, middlings often have trouble with fae food," one girl sniffed. "If it isn't properly enchanted, it can be quite a nasty experience." She grinned. "Well, you might as well be eating dust and spiders, hadn't you? And we thought it wouldn't be fair of us to let you dine as we do, not when you could end up with a mouthful of scorpions in the courts. It's only *loyal* of us to give you an honest experience. We wouldn't want you to think you could trust any fae feast you encountered, would we?"

Spiders? Scorpions? I put my plate down with a clatter. The other girls smirked.

Definitely not free from their spite, then.

"So, either you've enchanted my food, or you've enchanted yours?" I asked flatly. "Isn't that forbidden? A teacher is probably on their way here now to punish you all for casting a spell."

"*We* didn't enchant it," one girl said with an innocent expression. "Inara gets packages of treats from her mother back at court. I suppose it only tastes good to those of proper fae blood. A middling can't taste the magic. And they can't catch us for a spell we didn't perform."

"And you won't say anything," another girl added. "You wouldn't betray the loyalty of your Briar sisters by snitching, would you?"

I ground my teeth together.

"Marit," another girl said, this one tall and willowy, with curly black hair, drooping velvety ears, and pale white freckles across her dark brown skin like spots on a fawn. "Didn't I hear that you have six weeks of detention scrubbing the library floors for distributing charmwine on society night?"

Marit's face turned a shade of purple that made me fear for my safety, oath or not.

"Our new recruits can do it for me," she said loftily. "It'll be a good reminder about snitching."

The newest girls, all of whom seemed to know that it was somehow my fault, turned to me with glares of fury.

I rose and left the room without a word. I wasn't going to sit there and pretend I didn't notice their abuse, and I was tired of acting brave.

I stalked from the house, heading for the North Tower. My eyes stung.

The door creaked behind me.

"Wait," a voice called.

I turned and saw the girl with the white freckles. She jogged to catch up to me, and a grin brushed across her lips.

"I'm sorry for stirring the pot," she said. "I couldn't help myself. You rattle Marit, and she needs rattling. She's too comfortable with her status as queen of the snobs."

Up close, I could see that she had dark brown eyes like a doe's.

"I'm Elome," the doe-eyed girl said, reaching out one hand like an offering of goodwill. "I'm pleased to have you in our society, Kyra."

I hesitated, looking at her outstretching hand. Was this a trick? Another spider threat? Slowly, I put my palm in hers. Elome gave my hand a squeeze. No spiders.

"El-o-mee," I repeated, sounding out her name. "Hi."

"We aren't all snobs," she said with a laugh. "At least, not as snobby as the triplets and their ilk. I suppose I am a bit snobby, being elite."

I flushed. "I didn't mean to imply that all elite—"

"Relax," she said. "It's mostly true anyway." She studied me. "What court do you hail from?"

"The summer court," I murmured, feeling embarrassed as usual, like I was lying. I felt like an imposter to claim it.

Elome's brows lifted. "No wonder Marit hates you," she said. "She'd give anything to be from one of the seelie courts."

With that mysterious statement, she turned and headed back for the house, leaving me standing there. When she reached the door, she glanced over her shoulder and gave me another smile.

"I think you're going to make a fine addition to Briar," she said. "But don't tell the others I said so. I'll deny it."

With that, she slipped inside.

I turned on my heel and returned to the North Tower, my head spinning.

CHAPTER TWENTY-FIVE

"ELOME?" LYRICA INHALED in astonishment. "She's a princess from the autumnal court! You've made a politically powerful friend!"

"To be fair," Tearly interjected, "the autumnal court has a lot of princesses, since the king has twelve wives."

"Thirteen," Hannah corrected automatically. "And half of the wives have consorts of their own. It's a polyamorous situation."

"Still," Lyrica said, her eyes wide. "She's a good person to make friends with."

"I don't know that we're *friends*," I protested. "She seemed more pleased about the fact that Marit seems to hate me than anything else. But she was nice to me, I guess."

We were sitting on my bed, eating the cupcakes Lyrica and Tearly had brought back from their meeting. Apparently, the others girls' introductions to their societies had gone well. Dewdrop had served cupcakes and sang songs the whole time, and Flameforge had made all their new members climb a cliff and jump into the river. Both Lyrica and Hannah were thrilled.

I was just relieved to have the taste of dirt out of my mouth.

"And I'm on the student council now," I said, licking a crumb from my finger. "Is that good or bad?"

"Well, in most of the societies it's a coveted position," Tearly explained. "But you have to go to meetings and do a lot of extra work. Naturally, lazy elites don't want any part of it."

"Do we have any power?"

"Not really," Tearly said with a shrug. "You listen to student complaints, plan events, solve disputes, and fix problems around the school. Except the council usually doesn't get much done, because they can't come to any kind of consensus. Any new measures have to have five votes to pass, and good luck getting that kind of agreement from everybody."

"Wonderful," I muttered. "I wish I'd joined Stormtongue. I bet they had tea and a nice debate for their induction ceremony. Or Dewdrop. Hell, I'd be happier in Toadcurdle, I bet."

"Have another cupcake," Lyrica said in sympathy.

I took the confection from her gratefully. These cupcakes were less elaborate than the ones from society night—they were topped with lifelike flowers made from spun sugar—but they tasted just as delicious, and I was hungry and nervous for the future.

What had I gotten myself into?

~

The first student council meeting was held the next day in the bottom level of the library. I arrived early, not wanting to enter to a wall of stares, and found Toadcurdle's representative already sitting at the table with his hands folded in front of him. He wore thick eyeglasses that were rimmed in brass and looked like something from a steampunk cosplay. His hair was reddish brown, his skin was the color of amber, and he had impossibly long fingers.

"Hello," he said jovially as I took a seat. "I'm Gill. You're the middling that got into Briar, aren't you?"

"Kyra," I said, and I sighed. "And yes."

Gill appeared sympathetic. "What made you do it?" he whispered.

"Spite," I replied, and he chuckled.

The library door opened, and two more representatives entered. A curvy girl with silvery hair carrying a binder stuffed with pages, and a boy with eyes like a snake. They sat down and introduced themselves. The girl was from Stormtongue, the boy from Flameforge. Their names were Fallon and Iain.

Dewdrop was next, and its representative, Lula, was as sweet as one of its famed cupcakes. She had pink hair and big, blinking eyes. She sat next to me nervously, as if she wasn't sure what I was going to do if she got too close. She was also carrying a binder stuffed with pages.

The Basilisk chair sat empty, and we waited. Finally, Iain sighed as if he wasn't surprised and suggested we begin our meeting.

"Can't," Fallon said primly. "It's against the rules."

"We'll be waiting all day," he argued.

I got the sense this was a common disagreement between them.

Just then, the door opened, and the Basilisk representative strode inside.

My stomach dropped.

It was Lucien.

His dark gaze swept over me without stopping. He pulled out a chair and sat without a word.

"You're late," Fallon said.

Lucien shot her a glower, and she apparently decided not to press the issue further.

"First item of business," she said, opening her binder to the first page. "I've catalogued all of the things that we should attempt to accomplish this year—"

"Of course," Iain interrupted. "Let me guess. You want the wishing well bricked over, and the paths into the forest closed off, and the labyrinth filled with dirt?"

"First years keep filling the well with junk," Fallon exclaimed. "And someone is always getting lost on the forest paths. It's a looming threat. And don't get me started on the labyrinth—"

"We have to have a little risk in life," Iain argued. "If you had your way, we'd all be locked up in the school with spells all around and nothing to do but study and look out the heavily charmed windows."

"And what's wrong with that?" Fallon shot back. "Spellwood is dangerous—"

"And it's meant to be," a voice interrupted.

We looked up and saw a woman dressed in the billowing school robes of a teacher approaching us. She had hair the color of kelp and webbed ears that reminded me of fins on a fish. Her eyes were bright and restless, like jewels. I recognized her as Professor Yuri, who taught classes for the elite track. She was from the water court, and in addition to her professor duties, led swimming classes in the lake and rivers around the school.

"Hello, Professor Yuri," Fallon said in a tone that was less than hospitable. "I see you are still sentenced to student council duty."

"Hello, Fallon." The professor took her place at the head of the table with a sigh that spoke volumes about her enthusiasm for student council duty. "I see you have managed to get elected for a fourth time."

Fallon folded her hands. "I was unanimously voted in."

Professor Yuri rubbed a hand across her eyes. "And yes, Spellwood is dangerous. A little danger in a safe setting is necessary for the students to learn to navigate the perilous courts that await them at home, especially our mostly-mortal students. If we pad every corner and spell every step, they might be safe here, but what about when they leave?"

"Agree to disagree," Fallon said, jutting out her sharp chin.

I got the feeling Professor Yuri and Fallon disagreed a lot as well.

"But," Fallon added before anyone else could speak, "surely even you can see the prudence in closing the labyrinth? It's a death trap. Nobody is allowed down there anymore. Not after what happened—"

Professor Yuri's gaze sharpened.

"Even I know when to move on from a dead horse, Fallon," she said. "Let's continue with the agenda, shall we? Summertide. Who's in charge of the maze?"

"Dewdrop," Fallon announced with a frown. "As usual."

After what happened? Curiosity rose in me, sharp and insistent. I needed to know about all the dangers here at Spellwood.

To my disappointment, nobody said anything else about the labyrinth.

CHAPTER TWENTY-SIX

SUMMERTIDE DAWNED BRIGHT and clear, which Lyrica said the water court would be sad about. Apparently, they fervently hoped every year for a rainstorm. The air was hot and still, the morning heavy with anticipation of the holiday.

While we brushed our teeth and changed out of our pajamas, Hannah and Lyrica tried to explain Summertide to me.

"It's the longest day of the year," Lyrica said. "The fae—particularly the sun court and other seelie courts—have feasts and bonfires to commemorate it. My mother always invites every single one of my cousins, and they dance all night long. Everyone catches fireflies and makes small wishes, and then we leave sweets outside the front door in case the wisps overheard, because if they hear your wishes and then you leave them food, the wisps might grant your desires."

"Is it real?" I asked. "The wishes, I mean? Do they come true?"

Hannah shrugged and grinned. "Sometimes."

"Can you wish for anything?"

"No," Lyrica said. "And they don't last forever. One year I wished for black hair, and it was the color of a raven's wing all summer long, but then it turned green, and I had to cut it all off."

"Like Anne Shirley," I said, and thought of Lucien and his books with a funny feeling in my stomach.

"Who?" Lyrica said.

"It's a mortal thing," I said.

"Oh," Lyrica added. "Everyone carries things in their pockets that remind them of the people they love most. I'm going to be carrying a letter from my parents and a lock of my sister's hair. What about you?"

"I don't know," I said, thinking of my lost locket. "I suppose I could carry a letter—"

A knock at the door interrupted us. Hannah opened the door and found a palm-sized envelope lying on the ground.

"Oooh," she cried, and snatched it up. "A spellogram!"

"What's a spellogram?" I asked.

Both of my roommates looked at me, and then each other.

"You open it," Lyrica said.

I accepted the envelope and turned it over in my hand. A dab of blue wax sealed the paper.

"It's a haunter," Hannah murmured to Lyrica.

I slid my fingernail underneath the wax to break the seal, and the envelope snapped open like a trap. Sparks exploded from the paper and swirled up toward the ceiling. I dropped the envelope with a shriek.

A blue ghost screamed forth from the volley of sparks, its mouth gaping wide and its arms outstretched. It shot up and vanished in a cloud of smoke.

"What WAS that?" I gasped, both hands clutched to my chest.

Lyrica clapped her hands in delight. "A spellogram! The haunters are my favorite!"

"It's a little piece of charmed paper," Hannah explained when she'd wiped the tears of laughter from her eyes. "They're only allowed on holidays, since they're charms, but they're just harmless illusions. I bet Tearly sent it."

We found a giggling Tearly waiting at the bottom of the staircase, a hand clapped over her mouth.

"I could hear the screams from here," she said with a laugh, swatting at the crumpled up spellogram that I threw at her head. "Come on, let's get breakfast."

There was no school, and the students roamed the campus in groups, released spellograms and shot off poppers full of flower petals, and played bowling games in the gardens. Decorations had appeared overnight—round, golden lanterns were strung everywhere, and lush greenery twined across the windows and doorways and in arches over the paths. The whole school buzzed with excitement, and the feeling was infectious.

Lyrica was practically skipping as we walked to the dining hall for breakfast.

"Later tonight," she said, "there will be feasts, and roasted nuts and fruit on sticks, and of course, the maze."

"Maze?" I asked.

"The Summertide maze is a tradition," Hannah explained. "My grandfather's annual mazes were always the best at our court."

"And of course, the gowns," Lyrica added. "And we can use charms on ours because it's a holiday!"

Lyrica had been planning her dress for weeks, and even Hannah had been drawn into the fervor. They'd begged me to let them style me, and I'd agreed with nervous anticipation. I had no idea what I'd be wearing to the celebrations that evening.

"You're going to love your dress," Lyrica assured me. "I'm so excited."

We reached the main buildings and stopped to stare. A maze had sprouted seemingly overnight on the great lawn, made of bloodbrambles, the same thorny bushes that crawled up the sides of the main school buildings. It was so big that I couldn't see the end.

"How far does it go?" I asked as we skirted the edge of the maze on our way to the dining hall.

"You'll have to find out tonight!" Lyrica called in delight, dancing ahead of us up the steps of the main building.

I felt someone watching me, and I turned in time to see Lucien slipping away around a corner. I might have tried to follow him, but then someone set off a round of spellograms on the path, a whole host of haunters that screamed and swirled toward the sky in a cacophony of shrieks, and then Lyrica and Hannah dragged me inside to get our own spellograms from the school office, where they were passing envelopes out like candy.

I didn't see Lucien again.

~

We spent the rest of the morning and early afternoon ambushing each other with spellograms and playing a fae game on the lawn that reminded me of chess, if the chess pieces were made from large stones that had to be dragged into place with leather slings. In the evening, when dusk approached, we returned to the North Tower to get ready for the night celebration.

My dress was still a mystery to me. The girls made me close my eyes to get dressed. They wanted a big reveal.

"Okay, open your eyes," Hannah said, and I dropped my hands from my face and looked down at my Summertide gown.

"What do you think?" Lyrica demanded. "Did I do a good job?"

A gown of soft green and gold silk fell in asymmetrical folds to my knees. The bodice was green with gold roses creeping up it and wrapping around my left shoulder and arm in a single, cunning sleeve. The roses spilled down the skirt, transforming into a shower of silken petals that shimmered and rippled as I turned.

"It's amazing," I whispered, running my fingertips across the fabric.

Lyrica beamed. She was dressed in green and violet, with butterflies spelled across her skirt. Their wings fluttered as she moved. "Summertide dresses need to be good for dancing and running through mazes. And of course, the roses were a must. This way, everyone will remember that you're Briar. We won't let the bastards forget." She added in a pleased tone, "Hannah told me that's what mortals call annoying people. It doesn't always mean they are illegitimately born."

"Right," I said, laughing.

Hannah wore a shiny black jumpsuit with a long over-dress that fell almost to her ankles. The edges of the fabric flamed and smoked as if they were on fire, but they never burned up.

"Look," Lyrica said to me as she fussed with my skirt, "there are pockets for your lucky things that remind you of the people you love most. Right here, amid the folds. Isn't that cunning? Sometimes people forget to include them, and then they have to wear little bags around their necks called pocket necklaces. But you'll have the real thing."

"Thank you," I said. I still wasn't sure what I was going to put in my pockets to represent my mom and Grandmother Azalea. My gaze fell on the shelf above my bed, where I'd placed the things they'd given me before I came: my mom's dagger in its jeweled scabbard, and my grandmother's jewel-leafed necklace and bottle filled with purple shards of crystal.

I selected the knife for my mom and the necklace for my grandmother and placed one in each pocket.

"Enough hanging around," Lyrica said impatiently after we'd admired each other's outfits for a few minutes. "Let's get to the celebration!"

The sunlight had turned a drowsy golden-orange when we left the tower. The air was warm and still, and music drifted from the direction of the great lawn. The sound of it filled me with the itch to dance, and I remembered society night and felt a thrill of foreboding.

But no. I was safe now. I was a member of Briar, and nobody would mess with me. I'd stay with my friends and away from anything that might be charmwine.

The golden lanterns decorating the campus had already be lit, and they glowed above our heads as we reached the festivities. The doors of the school were thrown wide open, and music spilled outside along with the sounds of laughter and chatter.

Bonfires flickered along the paths, and students clustered around them, dressed in loose, glittering finery.

Tearly spotted us from where she stood beside one of the bonfires, her expression anxious, and she rushed over to link arms with me.

"There you are," she said. "I've been waiting and waiting."

She was dressed in a two-piece dress of dark gray that showed a strip of her stomach above a silver sash. The folds swirled like mist as she moved, and silvery blossoms fell to the ground in her wake.

"Tearly, stop stressing about the maze," I said, because I hadn't missed the anxiety still sparkling in her eyes. "It's going to be killer."

"I hope so," she said, brushing her fingers across her eyes. "Everything hangs on this."

"Remember how worried you were about society night?" Hannah adds. "And think about how amazing those cupcakes turned out."

"I guess so," Tearly murmured. She gave me an extra squeeze. "I'm a worried mess. I'm sorry."

"Let's eat," Lyrica said, pointing at the open doors to the school. "It's Kyra's first Summertide ever, and we have to do everything."

Long tables were laid out with a feast inside the dining hall. All the small tables and chairs had been cleared away to make room for a banquet of roasted game hens, fresh greens, piles of fruit, and bowls dripping with sweet and savory sauces.

We piled our plates high with food and went back outside to eat on the steps. As the sun sank beneath the trees and the day deepened into evening, the music played on, and the bonfires burned higher, piled with scented wood that smelled delicious and magical. Students danced around the fires. Fireflies winked in the darkness, and we watched as everyone got up to catch them in paper boxes.

"Here," Tearly said, handing me one of the paper containers. "Make a wish, friend."

I rose and stepped into the fragrant, warm darkness in search of a firefly. I knew what I'd wish—I'd wish to see my mom and Grandmother Azalea again, or at least get a letter from them. It'd been weeks since I'd heard from them, and homesickness clutched at my chest briefly as I went in search of a firefly.

I found one hovering at the entrance to the maze, blinking. It flew just out of my reach as I tried to catch it with the paper box, and then, before I could try again, someone jostled me out of the way and scooped it up while I stumbled backward into the brambles of the outer wall of the maze. Thorns scratched at my arms and tugged on my dress.

I looked up and saw Griffin standing in front of the entrance to the maze, framed by the brambles and the glow of the bonfires. Golden, beautiful Griffin, but there was a hardness in his eyes that I hadn't seen before. I didn't know how I'd missed it. He had a cruelty to him, I realized. He'd been using me all along, but I didn't understand why. Did all elites like to taunt middling students? Or did I put out some kind of vulnerable, confused vibe that drew them to me like sharks to the scent of blood?

Griffin smirked at me. "Sorry. Did you want that one?" He held out the box, and when I looked at it, he snatched it away.

I was going to wish that he'd wake up bald, I thought darkly.

"I don't want anything from you," I said.

"Such spirit. No wonder you've driven my brother mad," he said.

I didn't understand what he meant. "I haven't done anything to Lucien," I snapped, and moved to brush past him.

He caught my arm, pulling me back.

"Be careful," he said in my ear. "There are people who want you dead."

Fear skittered down my spine. I yanked my arm from his grasp. "What are you talking about? What do you know?"

"Oh, I've heard rumors," he said with a shrug and another maddening smirk. "Who've you managed to piss off this time, mortal girl?"

He strode away, laughing, before I could answer.

"Wait," I called, following him with a hissed curse under my breath. "What have you heard?"

But he wove into the crowd of students and disappeared.

I turned a full circle, looking for him, but he was gone.

I looked for my friends, but they'd moved from the steps, probably in search of fireflies. I felt suddenly lonely. I walked toward one of the bonfires, stopping to accept a stick of sugar-glazed fruit from someone who was passing them out. I held the stick out to the flames, and the person next to me glanced over and then smiled.

Elome.

"Nice dress," she said. "But you'd better not eat that."

I glanced down at my stick of fruit, which was sizzling from its proximity to the flames. "Why not?" I asked, uncertain.

"I heard someone spiked them with charmwine," she said. "Can you smell it? And look at the other students."

I tossed my fruit into the flames at once. She was right. All around us, students were giggling, their faces flushed by the heat of the bonfire. At first, I thought they were laughing at me, and then I realized, they were all charmed.

It wasn't a prank directed at me. It was a prank directed at the entire school.

I spotted Hannah a short distance away, a stick in her hand that was noticeably empty of fruit.

"Thanks," I said to Elome before I started toward Hannah, who looked a little loopy. "Hannah?"

"Kyra," she said, grinning at me. "There you are. Did you catch a fish?"

"A... what?" I asked.

"Er, I mean, did you make a firefly? Er... make a wish?"

"No," I said, studying her face. "Do you feel all right? How much firefruit did you eat?"

Hannah smiled blissfully and grabbed my hand, ignoring my question. "Let's dance. I love this music."

She was definitely drunk on charmwine.

"Maybe we should get you back to our room," I said, feeling a faint sense of panic. Mortals were susceptible to commands when drunk on charmwine, so Hannah was vulnerable right now.

"Not without Lyrica," Hannah protested. "I'll be lonely."

Lyrica. Not mortal, but not elite either. Would she be affected like Hannah?

I spotted Tearly across the lawn, carrying a plate of cupcakes. "Stay here," I told Hannah, and headed toward Tearly.

"Where's Lyrica?" I called to her above the music.

Tearly pointed toward the entrance of the school, and the plate balanced in her other hand wobbled. "She went inside a few minutes ago. What's wrong?"

"Did you have any of the firefruit?" I demanded.

"I had two," Tearly said. "It was delicious. Why?"

Oh no.

"Everyone is drunk on charmwine," I said. "Someone spiked the firefruit."

"What?" Tearly exclaimed, her eyes going wide.

"I've got to find Lyrica..." I looked around and didn't see her. And where was Hannah? She'd disappeared.

"I just saw Hannah, and she's vanished," I said, spinning to scan the crowd again.

This was turning into a nightmare.

"There she is," Tearly said, pointing.

I spotted my roommate dancing beside one of the bonfires with the sly-faced friend of Lucien's, the one named Tryst.

So, this was Lucien and his friends' trick? Another Basilisk joke at the expense of some middlings? Fury burned in my chest. They wouldn't humiliate her like they tried to humiliate me. I wouldn't let them.

I marched across the lawn and grabbed Hannah, pulling her away from Tryst. She made a sound of protest, and Tryst scowled at me.

"Hey, I was dancing with her," he said, and I saw that his face was flushed too.

They were both drunk on charmwine.

198

"Back off," I snarled at him. "Leave her alone. Don't bother her again."

"What's with you?" Hannah said in confusion and annoyance. "He isn't bothering me. I asked him to dance."

"Come on," I persisted, dragging Hannah toward the garden. "The Summertide celebration is over."

All around us, students staggered and giggled and danced frantically.

Where were all the teachers? The headmaster?

"Summertide is over?" Hannah asked. She tugged at my hand as she dug her heels into the ground. "But we haven't even caught our fireflies yet—"

"We'll catch fireflies from the window in our room," I said.

Tearly intercepted us. "I just saw Lyrica."

I turned and caught a glimpse of the fae girl at the steps of the school, surrounded by students in various states of drowsiness or giddiness. Again, I wondered where all the teachers were.

A golden figure appeared at the top of the steps above Lyrica.

Griffin.

My chest tightened.

"Stay with Hannah," I instructed Tearly, who was beginning to act giddy too. "I'll be right back. Don't go anywhere."

They looked at me with blank smiles.

"Stay," I repeated firmly, and then I ran toward Lyrica and Griffin.

I reached Lyrica before Griffin could. I grabbed her arm and pulled her down the steps with me. "Come on," I called over my shoulder.

She followed me without protest. She had a cupcake clutched in one hand. "Where are we going?"

"Back to Tearly and..." I frowned.

There was Tearly, but now where had Hannah gone?

This was worse than herding cats.

"Where is Hannah?" I asked with a note of panic in my voice when we reached Tearly.

"She went into the maze," Tearly said dreamily. "She heard someone calling her name."

"Who?" I demanded.

"Some Basilisk boy," Tearly said.

A Basilisk boy.

Hannah was far more mortal than Lyrica or Tearly, and thus more vulnerable while under the influence of charmwine. They could make her do anything.

I made a decision.

"Here." I planted Lyrica's unresisting hand in Tearly's. "Go back to the tower. Eat some snacks and wait for me and Hannah."

With that, I turned and plunged after Hannah into the maze.

CHAPTER TWENTY-SEVEN

THE INTERIOR OF the maze was filled with shifting shadows. The music and laughter from outside seemed oddly muffled, like I was underwater instead of just behind a few hedges of brambles. Perhaps some spell was at work keeping the sound at bay.

"Hannah?" I called out.

I listened, but nobody replied. I kept moving, running into a dead end and doubling back to the fork in the maze and taking the other path. All the while, I listened for the sound of Hannah's laughter.

Footsteps sounded on the other side of one of the hedges. I ran toward them. "Hannah? Hannah!"

I rounded a turn and collided full-force with another body. I fell backward on the matted grass.

Not Hannah.

"Lucien," I hissed in astonishment. He'd been the one to lure her inside the maze?

He stared down at me a moment, then offered me a hand up.

I ignored it and scrambled to my feet. "Where's Hannah?"

"Your roommate? Haven't seen her," he responded.

He wore a long gray cloak that made him blend with the shadows, and he was carrying one of his books in one hand. He wasn't dressed for the Summertide party. He looked like he was dressed to hide.

I waited for him to shove past me, but he only rocked on his heels and studied my face.

"Are you all right?" he asked then.

"Someone spiked all the firefruit with charmwine," I said. "It doesn't take much to guess who that might have been." I leveled a glare at him, and Lucien raised his eyebrows.

"Not me, if that's what you're implying," he said. "I've been in the maze all evening, reading."

"Why?" I spat, not believing him.

"I supposed you could say Summertide is my least favorite holiday," he said. "I like to make myself scarce. As a prince of the dark court, I'm sometimes seen as a target for lingering grudges on this day."

I thought of what I'd heard about Griffin's mother, the sun court queen, and her hatred for him. I had to admit it made sense for him to lay low.

"Well, someone in Basilisk did it."

"Not likely," Lucien said with infuriating confidence. "Basilisk was punished severely for what happened the last time. Nobody would've been interested in tempting the headmaster's wrath again, not so soon."

"Oh really? Who else could it be?" I said angrily. "Move out of my way; I don't have time for this. I have to find Hannah before someone tries to make her dance like a monkey—or worse." Tears rose in my eyes. I blinked hard to force them away. I wouldn't cry in front of him.

Lucian's hand closed over my wrist.

"Wait," he said.

I braced myself and prepared to yank away.

"Do you want me to help you look?" he said.

I looked at him in astonishment. I didn't answer. I was too startled. I just started forward on the path again, and after a pause, Lucien followed.

I didn't know what to say to him.

"So, you're talking to me again?"

"It's complicated," he said.

"Complicated? Disdain for mortals and middlings is hardly complicated. It's classist bigotry, and it's disgusting."

"It doesn't have anything to do with you being a middling," he replied with a note of surprise in his voice. "Did you think that it did?"

"What else could it be?"

He didn't answer. He studied me as if seeing something for the first time before I brushed past him to keep looking.

I didn't have time for this.

The path abruptly ended in a round outdoor room bordered by hedges with a pond in the center. Another dead end. No sign of Hannah.

I whirled to head back the way I'd come, and Lucien blocked my path.

"Kyra," he said, and this time he sounded desperate. "Wait."

My eyes shot to his. His use of my name made me shiver. It made me feel seen, exposed. I didn't know what to make of it.

"We need to find Hannah," I said.

"What happened with Basilisk..." Lucien shook his head as his eyes sparked with sudden anger that took me by surprise. "That wasn't about you being a middling. It was a cruel taunt meant to hurt me, and me alone. I'm sorry it happened to you—it was vile for them to use you like a plaything. I just... I just wanted to say that."

203

I absorbed his apology with a nod.

"What do you mean, a cruel taunt meant to hurt you?"

Lucien's jaw tightened at the question.

"We should find your friend," he said instead of answering, and moved past me.

It was my turn to grab his arm to stop him. "Why?" I demanded, but my voice came out as a whisper instead of the strong tone I'd been going for. "Is it because they tried to get me to... to kiss you? Am I that repulsive?"

We were standing close together. I could see a vein pulsing in his throat.

He removed my hand from his arm and brushed past me. "We should find your friend."

I followed him, my heart beating fast.

Shadows coated the paths, making it difficult to see. Fireflies danced in the brambles just out of reach, and moonlight glowed overhead, casting faint light. I paused at another fork in the maze, mentally reviewing the paths I'd already tried.

"This way," I said, although I wasn't sure. I cupped my hands around my mouth. "Hannah!"

Silence.

I started down the darkened path, the one I hadn't tried yet. This must be the way.

Lucien followed.

The brambles pressed closer as the path narrowed, and they began to bloom giant, sweet-smelling white flowers as we passed. The effect was stunning, but I barely noticed.

"Hannah!" I called again.

We came to another dead end, another outdoor room, this one made to look like a cathedral, with the brambles twisted into thick thorny pillars and arching windows, with even a dome overhead laden with the white flowers. Stone monoliths ringed the center of the space, and a mossy stone statue of a dragon stood in the center, its clawed feet braced and its wings outstretched as if it were about to take flight.

Through the windows I saw the bonfires on the lawn, and several teachers herding charmwine-drunk students toward the buildings.

I halted, frustrated. I was certain this was the path forward. Had I missed a direction?

"Look," Lucien said, pointing past me. "Isn't that your friend?"

I turned and looked where he was pointing, through one of the high windows formed by the brambles, and saw Hannah standing beside one of the bonfires with Professor Quaddlebush, who was gesturing toward the North Tower. He shook a finger at her, and she reached out a hand and bopped his nose. Beside her, Tryst howled with laughter.

She was fine. Everything was fine. Relief rushed through me like a gust of wind.

"How did we miss her in the maze?" I looked at Lucien, who stood in the shadows of the path, his book dangling from his hand, studying me with an expression I couldn't decipher.

Now that my frantic search for Hannah was over, I hesitated.

"Why?" I asked. "Why would Griffin torment me to hurt you?"

Lucien turned his head toward mine. The moonlight glinted along his sharp cheekbones and winked across his antlers. His eyes were dark with sudden vulnerability, and his mouth opened, but he said nothing.

Emboldened, I stepped forward until I was almost in front of him. My heart thudded.

"You like me," I said. It was almost an accusation as it tumbled out. "Don't you?"

"No," Lucien said. "Of course not."

He didn't sound remotely convincing.

"You do. Are you ashamed to be attracted to a middling? Is this like with Darcy and Elizabeth in *Pride and Prejudice*, where I'm from an inferior family that would be an embarrassment to your good breeding, and you'd never stoop so low—"

"It isn't like that," he hissed. "Don't pretend you don't know."

"Know what?"

We were close. So close we were almost touching.

He turned his head away.

"You think I don't know that you're hiding your heritage, but I saw the golden flash in your eyes that night we went into the forest."

"What flash? What does that mean?" I didn't understand.

"It was right after we left the forest. I brushed your hair from your face. Do you remember?"

I remembered—after that night, he'd been cool and remote—but it didn't explain anything. "Help me out here, Lucien. I'm a mostly mortal. A middling. I'm new to all of this."

He exhaled. "Are you really going to play this game?"

"I'm not playing a game," I insisted.

He gave me a look that bordered on exasperation. "You have sunshine in your blood. The sun court. You are poison for me. And yet, you try to seduce me."

A laugh burst out of me.

206

. the sun court. Second—
yourself."
                      :ven to me.
       Lu   ard, backing me against one
of the co.   nedge cathedral. I sucked in a
breath as he .   close to me.

"Why are you u.ing this?" he breathed. "Why are
you tormenting me?" His lashes brushed his cheeks
as he lowered his eyes to my lips.

"I'm not from the sun court." My heart beat fast
as gaze tangled with mine once more. "And I haven't
done anything to you."

"The first time I saw you standing on the path, it
was like a sword through my heart."

"I haven't done anything," I retorted, feeling a
little dizzy.

"No?" he countered. His eyes were the color of
summer moss in the moonlight. "You ask me about
my past, my books. Pretend an interest in me. Hum
songs in the Cistern that remind me of something I
can't explain. Wear my royal colors, even."

"I don't even know what that last one means." I
ducked from beneath his arm and put distance
between us.

"Green for my mother's house, gold for my
father's," Lucien said. "In the fae courts, it's a sign
of affection. Intention to attract, even."

"These are my favorite colors," I said. "They make
me feel safe and happy, and they have since I was a
little kid. It has absolutely nothing to do with you."

"No? You flirt with my brother in front of me," he
continued.

"Only until I discovered what a jerk he is. And
wait a second. I made up that song in the Cistern. It
isn't my fault if you liked it. I'm not playing a twisted

fae game, Lucien. This isn't the dark court. It's Spellwood. I'm not a fae assassin. I'm not some secret sun court enemy trying to hurt you."

He was silent. The wind blew a lock of his hair across his eyes. Moonlight glinted on the tips of his antlers, which were barely visible in his hair.

"Believe me," I whispered. "I'm just... me."

We were silent. Lucien's throat bobbed as he swallowed hard. His eyes were like dark embers, burning me, but in the best possible way.

I took a step back toward him. Something compelled me to be close to him, to reassure him that we were friends, not enemies. "Any other things that I've been doing that you want to bring to my attention?"

Lucien leaned against one of the stone monoliths. His mouth lifted in a half smile. "You stare at me all the time like you want to kiss me."

"I do not," I protested, flushing hot.

"You don't stare? Or you don't want to kiss me?"

Somehow, we were even closer now. His lashes lowered as he gazed down at me. I could feel the heat of his hands that were inches from mine.

"I don't want to kiss you about as much as much as you don't like me," I breathed, because I did want to kiss him. All at once, my stomach was in knots, and my hands were shaking, and I felt hot and cold at the same time.

"You don't understand," Lucien said again, his words pained. His breath brushed my lips, and the air between us tightened like an invisible cord. He searched my face as if looking for the answer to some vital question.

"Then explain it to me." We were so close.

"The sun court—"

"For the love of god, Lucien, I'm not from the sun court," I whispered.

"Indulge me a moment," he whispered. "If you did have sun blood in you, I couldn't let myself want you. You would be a danger to me. And I to you."

"I don't understand—your father was from the sun court," I said. "And here you are."

"My mother died giving birth to me," he said harshly. "Their union poisoned her and eventually killed her. It all started with a kiss."

"Why would I endanger myself?" I asked. "If I was from the sun court, you'd be a danger to me too. So why would I try to seduce you at risk to myself? Why would I want to be poisoned?"

That seemed to resonate with him. He thought that over for a moment.

"Do you believe me?" I pressed.

"Maybe." His gaze was guarded but cautiously hopeful now. "When Griffin was pursuing you, I thought he and you were working together to torment me."

"Does your brother always try to take things he thinks you like?"

"Yes," Lucien said, and closed his eyes briefly. "My brother often does such things."

My heart skipped a beat. How cruel.

He brushed his index finger against the side of my hand hesitantly, and I turned my palm over to meet him. He slid his hand over mine, and the place where our skin touched felt like a flame.

"You said..." I paused, flustered and a little light-headed. "You said you couldn't let yourself want me. Does that mean..." I continued in a small voice. "Does that mean that you do?"

I didn't know why I suddenly couldn't breathe as I waited for him to reply.

Lucien tipped his head back against the monolith. "Kyra. Something about you drives me mad. You're like something I didn't know I was missing."

"Lucien," I said.

His eyes snapped to mine.

"I'm not from the sun court. I'm not working with Griffin to hurt you. I'm not under the influence of charmwine. I can kiss whoever I want by my own free will."

"So, you do want to kiss me." His mouth curved in a wicked smile.

"I—"

That smile taunted me. I just wanted to make him stop smirking. I just wanted...

I wanted...

I kissed him.

CHAPTER TWENTY-EIGHT

LUCIEN'S HANDS CAME up to cup my jaw, and my fingers tangled in his hair as his mouth moved against mine. He tasted like summer nights and moonlight, and I kissed him back hard, hungry for him. He slid one hand down to rest on my hip and kept the other under my chin, lifting my face to his.

It was the best kiss I'd ever had.

As the kiss deepened, a spark of something electric leaped between us, making me dizzy. I put out a hand to brace myself against one of the hedge walls as my legs turned to jelly, and I sighed against his lips before pressing closer.

But Lucien stiffened as if coming to his senses. He pulled away from me, breathing hard, staring at me.

Visions of dark forests and stars in the night spun through my head like the aftertaste of a dream. The words of the wondering well ran through my head. *Sometimes, danger is found in delight, and delight in dark of night.*

Lucien brushed his thumb across my lower lip as his eyebrows furrowed. "Did you feel that?"

I nodded, still dizzy. "It was, ah, good."

"You have sun blood," Lucien said. "You lied to me."

"I didn't lie!"

We stared into each other's eyes, both of us confused and desperate. I wanted to make him understand. I wished I could let him see into my mind and my heart and know I wasn't trying to hurt him.

"And yet," Lucien murmured to himself, "Despite the danger, I still want to kiss you again."

"Lucien," I said, my voice thick and husky. "I'm not—I'm not trying to trap you, I swear—"

"Like the fool I am, I don't even care," he whispered, and leaned in to kiss me again.

And then I heard it.

A rumbling sound.

The ground beneath our feet quivered. The brambles around us thickened. All the gaps and windows disappeared as the vines smoothed into a wall, trapping us in a thorny cage, windowless. The cathedral effect was gone, replaced by something that looked more like a prison.

"What's happening?" I said as a quiver of fear lanced through me. "Is this something Summertide-related? Or is it because of you and me?"

"Neither," Lucien said, scanning the bramble walls. "This is something else—"

Before he could finish his sentence, the stone statue of the dragon twitched, groaned, and turned toward us.

The eyes glowed. With a guttural snarl, the stone dragon broke free from its pedestal.

"Is it supposed to do that?" I cried out, stumbling back.

"Run," Lucien urged, and he pushed me toward the path as the dragon statue lunged toward us with a roar like rocks grinding together.

I ran.

The bramble walls of the maze pressed closer as we fled down them. Vines snaked across our path, tripping us, coiling around our ankles before we broke away. The stone dragon hurtled after us, each step rumbling like a tiny earthquake as it lunged forward.

We reached a fork in the maze and went left only to run into a wall of brambles. The dragon loomed behind us, lashing its stone tail, eyes luminous as Summertide lanterns.

I looked frantically around me for a stick.

But would I be able to shove a stick through the chest of that solid stone creature?

"This way," Lucien gasped, grabbing my arm to yank me after him. There was a break in the wall that we hadn't seen in the shadows. We dodged a strike from the dragon and rushed through it.

The gap disappeared behind us in a snapping of vines and branches as the stone dragon plunged after us. The entire wall uprooted, thorns lashing at my heels as the dragon shook the vines loose from its neck.

The maze curved, and the path narrowed as the vines coiled like snakes.

"Someone must be manipulating it!" Lucien shouted to me.

We reached another fork in the maze. Both paths were tightening, the entrances shrinking like a drawstring pulling the mouth of a bag closed.

We burst through the one on the right. One of the vines caught my foot like the tentacle of a live creature, but I kicked free and kept running. Lucien caught me when I stumbled, and then we were hand in hand, fleeing through the dark.

I saw light at the end of the path—the exit—we'd nearly made it—

The stone dragon roared behind us. Something slammed into my leg, tripping me. I clawed my way back up with Lucien's help and lurched for the exit, my lungs straining to breathe, every cell in my body shouting at me to run.

We reached the entrance, but the stone dragon leaped over our heads and landed in front of us in a crouch, blocking our way.

Lucien pushed me behind him, but the beast knocked him aside with one swipe of its stone tail. He hit the ground, unconscious.

"Lucien!" I shouted.

The dragon turned its attention to me. I tried to run, but I was hemmed in on all sides by the broken remnants of the hedges.

I had to distract the dragon.

I remembered that I still had a single spellogram in my pocket. I yanked it out and ripped the seal open as the stone dragon raised its tail again to strike me down.

Blue sparks erupted from the paper as a spelled blue ghost screamed forward from the spellogram. The dragon reared up, startled, and another thought clicked dimly in my mind.

My pockets!

I had a dagger, the one from my mom.

I yanked the dagger free, tossed away the sheath, and hurled the blade straight at the beast's chest.

The blade collided with the stone dragon right below its neck. The dagger made a clanging sound as it struck the stone, as if I'd rung a bell.

A shockwave of magic rippled across my skin.

The stone dragon stumbled as cracks shot through its limbs and down its back. It let out a final roar and dissolved into dust and shards of rock.

214

I stood shaking, staring at where the monster had been before I tossed the rod aside and dropped to examine Lucien, who was still unconscious. A dark bruise colored the left side of his face, and blood dripped from his nose and down his chin. I turned his head carefully and pressed my ear to his mouth to listen for breathing.

"Lucien," I whispered, my voice trembling.

He was breathing. I exhaled in relief. Still, I was pretty sure he needed to see a doctor or healer or whatever mostly fae folk used for medical assistance.

I looked around and saw that we'd exited the maze on the opposite side of the great lawn from the party, near the old greenhouse where Briar had hosted their society party. The faint sounds of merriment echoed in the distance.

I was too far away to scream for help. I'd have to run to find it.

I staggered to my feet in time to see a figure approaching out of the darkness.

Tearly.

"Oh, thank goodness," I gasped. "Tearly! I'm so glad to see you. Something attacked us in the maze, and we almost didn't escape. Lucien's hurt, we need to..."

My voice trailed off into silence as she stepped closer, and I saw the bow and arrow she held, notched and ready to fire. Her face was pale and resolute as she pointed the tip of the arrow straight at my chest.

CHAPTER TWENTY-NINE

WAS SHE CONFUSED? Could she not see who I was in the dark?

"Tearly?" I tried again. "It's me. Kyra."

Tearly's eyes were dark as they met mine. She pressed her lips together, and my stomach tumbled like a stone as I realized. The words from the wondering well whispered through my head.

The killer is closer than you think.

No.

NO.

It couldn't be. It was impossible.

"You're a difficult one to kill," Tearly said, her voice strangely high, as if she was trying to sound brave and failing.

I stared at her. I didn't want to understand, but the realizations were clicking into place.

Tearly had designed the maze, the same maze that had just tried to kill me. She'd sent me inside to find Hannah, who had been by the bonfires the whole time, safe and happy.

The whole thing had been a trap, and I'd fallen into it.

"We're allowed to use spells on holidays without being immediately swooped upon by teachers," Tearly said as if reading the thoughts that must be apparent on my face. "It was a good plan, I thought. No would notice the use of magic that set the dragon statue in motion to attack you, or the way the maze closed up like a trap when you tried to run. Of course, you had the dark prince there to muck things up, and you always seem to get free somehow. I suspected you might, so I came here to wait in case the maze failed."

A shudder ran from my scalp to my toes.

"Were you the one who spiked the firefruit with charmwine?" I asked.

"A convenient reason to get you to look for Hannah," she said. "It's not the first time I've tried to kill you. I wanted to make certain it would work this time. That you'd actually go in the maze and look through the whole thing."

My mind spiraled with thoughts and revelations.

"The fragmyr," I breathed. "That was you?"

Tearly's mouth twitched. Her eyes darkened.

"I thought it would be quick," she confessed. "I summoned it outside the grounds where the magic wouldn't be detected and sent it for you. It was supposed to attack you while you walked home alone, but those creatures never do what they're made to do. It attacked you early, and it was no match for more than one person."

I swallowed hard. "Lucien said it wasn't big enough to be lethal anyway."

"Lucien," Tearly spat, "has gotten in the way too many times." She cast a glance at him lying unconscious on the ground as if debating whether to shoot him.

My ears rang with shock. She was my friend. My first friend at Spellwood. The one I trusted with my secrets, my embarrassments, my fears.

How could she do this? I thought I'd known her, but I was wrong. I had no idea who this cold killer standing before me was.

"What about the well?" I whispered. "When you bumped into me..."

"Yes. I forgot about that one. I didn't have the nerve then," she said. "I was supposed to push you in, make it look like an accident. But I couldn't do it."

"And the road? The bike accident? Was that you?" I rubbed at the place where the mark had been on my arm.

"What road? What bike accident?" Tearly said, genuinely confused. "That wasn't me."

She wasn't the only one trying to kill me? Or was she working for someone else? Was this a concerned effort with more than one killer?

"Are you even a student here?" I managed. "Are you even a half-blood? Or are you some professional fae assassin?"

"I'm a student," Tearly said. Her hand, I noticed, shook as it held the bow.

She was scared too.

"You don't have to do this, Tearly," I said. I thought of my mom's dagger, lying somewhere in the grass. Could I find it in time to stop her?

Her mouth tightened. "They picked me because of my family. Because I had access to you. They told me to befriend you and gain your trust, and then make   it   happen."

I had to do something to distract her. The words rushed out before I had time to think them through, and I hoped they'd be enough.

"You don't want to kill me," I whispered, looking at her pale face. "You've been making half-hearted attempts. The too-small fragmyr, the maze that didn't work quite right. You're going through the motions, but you don't want to succeed."

"I have a debt that must be repaid," Tearly cried out. "I am bound by the power of my name and by the oath of my blood to keep the debt. No, I don't want you dead. You're my friend. But they gave the orders, and I have to follow. I have to do what I'm told."

I could still hear the sounds of the party in the distance. Tearly heard it too; she took aim at my chest again.

I had to keep her talking.

"Who? Who really wants me dead? Who is making you do this?"

Tearly straightened, inhaling as if bracing herself for something she was dreading. "That doesn't matter now, Kyra. I couldn't tell you anyway."

"I can help you, Tearly," I tried. "Headmaster Windswallow can help you. Spellwood is safe. You'll be safe here—"

"You don't understand! Spellwood can't help me. And even if they could, my brother—"

She stopped.

"What happened to your brother?"

Tearly shook her head.

Lucien stirred on the ground with a groan. Tearly's eyes snapped to him and then back to me.

Her finger itched over the arrow as tears gathered in the corners of her eyes and slid down her face. "I'm sorry. You were my friend, Kyra, truly you were."

She was about to kill me.

I never quite understood what happened next, except that something inside me rose up and screamed NO. As the arrow left the bow, light erupted all around us, blinding me and enveloping Tearly. She screamed as if in pain, and the arrow missed me and landed harmlessly in the grass.

Lucien shouted my name, but I could barely hear him, for a buzzing sound filled my ears and rumbled through my blood like electricity. Faintly, I could make out cries of alarm in the distance, and then I heard Lucien call, "Over here!"

Then, the world around me went dark.

CHAPTER THIRTY

I WOKE IN Headmaster Windswallow's office, covered with a blanket.

The room was dark except for the flickering light from the Summertide bonfires coming through the windows. I lay across the same chairs where I'd been sentenced to detention with Lucien. The door was closed, and I could hear heated voices engaged in a debate outside it.

One of the voices sounded like my grandmother's. I sucked in a startled breath, pushed back the blanket covering me, and slid off the chairs. As I stood, I caught a glimpse of myself in the mirror that hung over the headmaster's desk.

My hair was threaded with glowing strands of gold. My eyes blazed like small suns. My skin had the faintest sheen when I loved, like I had glitter in my pores.

Shock rippled across my skin as I gazed at my reflection. My pulse thundered.

What had happened to me?

I crept to the door and put my ear against it to listen.

"She's going to find out eventually. It'll be better this way."

That was definitely Grandmother Azalea's voice.

I yanked open the door and ran into her arms with a cry. Tears filled my eyes as she hugged me tight against her.

More arms enveloped me. Mom. I closed my eyes and allowed myself to feel safe and whole for a moment.

Just a moment, though. That's all the time I allowed before I pulled away and unleashed the torrent of questions I had. "What's going on? How did you get here? Am I going to be expelled?"

Over their shoulders, I spotted Headmaster Windswallow striding toward us down the hall. Her expression was grim.

My stomach dropped.

I already had a reputation as a troublemaker. I'd already been given two detentions. Would they believe me when I explained what happened? Would Headmaster Windswallow be more inclined to listen with my mom and Grandmother Azalea watching?

How would I even begin to explain?

"Miss Solschild," she said. "If you would join us in my office, please."

I shot a glance at my mom and Grandmother Azalea before we followed the winged woman inside. She closed the door behind us and indicated that we should sit.

"What happened?" I asked, my lips numb. "Is Lucien okay? Is Tearly?"

The headmaster took a seat with a rustle of her feathers and studied me a moment across her broad desk. "What happened after you left the maze, Kyra?"

Did that mean Tearly was on the loose?

I licked my lower lip. "Tearly..." My voice trembled, and I shut my eyes and took a deep breath to steady it. "You've got to find her. Tearly drugged all of the other students with charmwine, and then she tried to kill Lucien and me. She's been secretly using charms to make attempts on my life. This was the latest one. She used the maze to trap us, and then she brought a statue to life and herded us to

222

where she was waiting with a bow and arrow. I know it sounds crazy, but—"

"Not so crazy, Miss Solschild." Headmaster Windswallow's tone was kind. "Help arrived just as she was letting loose an arrow at your heart. She was restrained immediately by your defense teacher, actually."

"Jor-Ass?" I was astonished. For some reason, I couldn't fathom him coming to my rescue.

"That's Sir Joras to you," Headmaster Windswallow corrected, but a smile hovered at the edges of her lips.

I wondered if I wasn't the first to call him that.

A sigh escaped me. "Did Tearly say anything? What will happen to her now? And what about Lucien?"

"Lucien is recovering well and seems to be uninjured. Tearly is currently awaiting the discipline of her court. She will be punished severely for her actions."

Lucien was safe. Tearly was... well, I couldn't think about that now. It made me want to curl into a ball and weep. I didn't have time for that right now. I had to figure out what was going on.

"Am I going to be expelled?" I whispered.

A brief smile touched Headmaster Windswallow's lips. "No, Miss Solschild. We do not expel students for using magic under life or death instances of self-defense. You acted bravely and saved both your life and that of Lucien. You shall be commended."

"Magic?" I managed, confused.

"Your summoning of light to confuse your attacker and signal to everyone at the party at the same time was brilliant, my dear," Headmaster Windswallow said. "Nonlethal and extremely effective. I'd heard you were a good student in your Danger and Defense class, and I believe it fully."

"But I didn't use magic," I interrupted. "I *can't* use magic. I'm a middling. A near mortal. I know you've punished me before for it, but... you were mistaken. I'm not capable of it."

Headmaster Windswallow looked at my mom and grandmother with her eyebrows raised.

"I see there are things the three of you still need to discuss," she said. "You may have use of my office as long as you need it."

"Thank you," Grandmother Azalea said.

The headmaster rose gracefully and went to the door. She paused and looked over her shoulder at me.

"Kyra," she said, "I'm proud of you."

When she'd gone, I looked at my mom and grandmother.

"What's going on?"

My mom swallowed and looked at her hands. "I'm afraid your grandmother and I are the ones who have been lying to you, Kyra."

"Omitting the truth," Grandmother Azalea said in a tone that suggested they'd had this argument over semantics before.

"Regardless," my mom said, "it's time you knew the truth. The full truth."

Her eyes glimmered with tears as she leaned forward and took my hands in hers.

"Your father wasn't just any fae," she said. "He was powerful in magic, and a political opponent of the king on the throne. When I was pregnant with you, he was killed—some said he was murdered, though it was never proven. I fled back to the mortal world to keep you safe, and told his family when they came looking that I'd miscarried you."

I stared at her, barely able to absorb everything she'd just told me.

My mom checked my expression carefully as if looking for horror or anger. Her brow wrinkled, and she paused, pressing her lips together the way she did when she was about to do something that made her nervous. "There's more. We... I... told you another untruth. I didn't want you to be recognized. I told the school—and you, so you wouldn't have to try to remember a lie or feel any worries about it—"

Grandmother Azalea laid a hand on my mom's arm. My mom took a deep, steadying breath.

"I told you before that your father was from the summer court. But that wasn't true. He... he was from the sun court."

The sun court? The royal court of the fae? The most powerful court of all? The sworn enemies of the dark court?

My world telescoped. I was speechless as my understanding of the world rearranged itself yet again.

My glowing hair. My golden eyes I'd glimpsed in the mirror.

My eyes...

Lucien.

Your eyes. They flashed golden.

He'd been right—and I'd sworn to him that he was wrong. I'd told him to trust me! He, from the dark court, when I was from the sun court.

"Don't be afraid," my mom said, probably taking my expression for one of alarm. "Your fae blood is strong. You have magical abilities, Kyra. Power. You defeated your attacker. You rescued yourself."

225

Did this mean I had accidentally attacked the student in my class? I hadn't been framed after all?

I shook my head. "Why have I never felt it before? Why have I never accidentally made something glow in the dark, or enchanted the dog? I don't understand."

My mom cleared her throat. "Your grandmother Azalea and I performed a few, ah, charms to keep them subdued and hidden. We didn't want to alarm you, or cause you to draw attention to yourself."

"You didn't tell me and you put charms on me." An unsettling feeling dropped over me like a weighted blanket. My stomach curdled as everything I'd thought I'd known to be true shifted a little more.

My mom winced but nodded. "Yes."

Grandmother Azalea lowered her head. "I'm sorry," she whispered. "I understand if you are angry with us. If you need... time."

Was I angry?

I couldn't tell what I was feeling. My dominant emotion at the moment was a numbness that I knew wasn't going to last. Sooner or later, my emotions would come crashing through.

At least right now, I had the luxury of clear-headedness.

"I don't think I'm angry," I said slowly, parsing out the words. "Not for myself, I mean. I... I guess I understand why you did it. But..." I thought again of Lucien. Our kiss. Could I have hurt him?

My mom and Grandmother Azalea watched my face, their expressions haggard. I wanted to hug them both and whisper that it was going to be okay.

Was it going to be okay?

Their lies had consequences.

226

Thinking about all of it made me feel a million years old, and tired.

"It was dangerous of you to lie to me," I said finally. "Dangerous for me, dangerous for other people. I'm not angry, I'm just, well, disappointed."

The joke was ignored.

My grandmother rubbed her forehead like she'd lost a year of her life waiting for my reaction, and my mom let out something between a sigh and a sob.

"I'm truly sorry, Kyra," she said.

"Anything else you want to tell me, since we're confessing secrets?" I said.

"Ask anything you like," Grandmother Azalea said. "We'll tell you the answer. I promise you."

I didn't even know where to begin. I was overwhelmed trying to sort through the mountain of questions piled on my brain.

I touched a strand of hair that shimmered in the light.

"Why do I look so... so golden?"

"It must be an element of the powers we were suppressing," my mom said. "When you used them, I guess you blasted to bits the charm that kept your true nature hidden."

"Am I going to look like this forever now?" I turned my arm back and forth, marveling at the faint twinkles of gold I saw playing across my skin. It was beautiful... and unnerving. How would I ever be able to go out in public in the mortal world? I looked like a cosplayer.

I certainly didn't look normal.

"Although charms are not normally allowed, we have permission from the headmaster to spell you again," my mom said. "Since it's for your safety. If you walk around looking like that, it might attract the kind of attention we're looking to avoid."

"My assassin?" I guessed.

She nodded.

I was glad. My new look would attract a lot of obvious attention that I wasn't sure I wanted.

Something else occurred to me, and I felt a fresh pang of alarm. "If I'm a princess, do you have a claim to the sun court's throne? Does that mean your life is in danger too, Mom?"

My mom shook her head. She brushed a hand across my cheek. "I was only a consort, and your father is no longer alive. The only royal blood in our family is you, Kyra."

"The king of the sun court..." My thoughts tumbled over each other as I put the pieces of what she'd told me together. "He isn't my father?"

"No. The sun king hails from a rival dynasty."

So, Griffin wasn't my brother or cousin or anything else that would make the fact that we kissed weird.

And Lucien wasn't related to me either.

But.

But, but, but.

Lucien was from the dark court. I was from the sun court.

Seelie and unseelie.

Light and dark.

I remembered the words from the lecture.

Dark extinguishes the light. Light devours the dark. They are forever opposed. Naturally at war.

I had to talk to him. I had to try to explain.

"Where is Lucien?" I said to my mom.

"Lucien?"

"The guy who was with me. The headmaster said he was being treated for his injuries or something. I need to see him."

"You need to rest," my mom said, and put a hand against my cheek.

"Who is this Lucien?" my grandmother muttered. "Are you seeing him?"

I bit my lip. "He's just a..." The word *friend* died on my lips. After tonight, I didn't know what he'd be.

"I need to talk to him and see that he's all right. Please—Mom, Grandmother Azalea."

My mom held my gaze a moment. "You can't tell anyone else about your father, Kyra. Or your secret heritage. It has to be a secret. Only Headmaster Windswallow and the other teacher who rescued you—Joras, was that his name? —can know."

A hollow pit opened in my stomach.

"Nobody else," my mom insisted. "It's too dangerous."

She was right. Lucien was from the dark court. I was attracted to him, and I might even like him, but I didn't know if I could trust him. I didn't know anything about him.

I wanted to tell him, but I couldn't. I'd already been attacked by one friend tonight.

I couldn't trust anyone at all.

"Kyra?" My mom waited for my reply.

I nodded and cleared my throat. "I won't tell anyone else."

"Good," my mom whispered, and pulled me tight in a hug. "I love you."

I gazed over her shoulder at the darkness outside. The bonfires glowed faintly in the distance even though the celebration was over. Summertide was past. I'd almost been assassinated by one of my best

229

friends, and been kissed by my natural mortal enemy, and I'd survived both.

What might be waiting for me tomorrow at Spellwood Academy?

ACKNOWLEDGEMENTS

My husband, Scott, for being the finest human being on this planet. You are my best friend and my favorite person. As Leslie Knope says, "I love you and I like you."

My sweet babies, who are getting funnier every day.

C and K, for watching the littlest one and keeping her safe and happy while I'm writing my books.

My family, for helping so much with my children and for supporting my dream however you can. Love you guys.

Dani Crabtree, for being an editing ninja of awesome and for writing funny and inspiring comments in the manuscripts you return to me. You're the best.

My readers, for your unflagging support and infectious enthusiasm. It means so much to me that you read my stories. I love you guys.

ABOUT THE AUTHOR

Kate Avery Ellison lives in Atlanta, Georgia, with her husband, two children, and two cats. She loves dark chocolate, fairy tale retellings, and love stories with witty banter and sizzling, unspoken feelings. When she isn't working on her next writing project, she can be found reading, watching one of her favorite TV shows, or lying on the couch in exhaustion due to her two rambunctious children under the age of three.

You can find more information about Kate Avery Ellison's books and other upcoming projects on her Facebook page, website, or Amazon author page.

WHILE YOU'RE WAITING FOR THE NEXT
SPELLWOOD BOOK...

Check out the first chapter of *Red Rider* by Kate
Avery Ellison

**Werewolves. A human resistance. And a girl
caught between two worlds.**

**Red Riding Hood meets The Handmaid's Tale
in this post-apocalyptic YA fairytale retelling!**

*In a land where a werewolf army called the
Sworn rule over the humans and walking corpses
called treecrawlers roam the wilderness between
settlements, orphaned Red has a secret that she
and her grandmother have been hiding for years.
She's one of the Chosen, the despised young
women selected to bear children in the stead of
barren female werewolves.*

*Red keeps her identifying mark hidden, and she
doesn't take advantage of the luxuries available
to the future mothers of the Sworn. But her secret
is discovered when she rescues her rebel
boyfriend from execution for treason, and she can
hide the truth no longer.*

*Red is intercepted by a dangerous young Sworn
named Vixor Rae, a prince among the
werewolves, and taken through the dangerous
wilderness to serve her fate in the capital.*

Vixor intrigues Red against her will, but he is her enemy, and she wants nothing more than to see him dead.

But when treecrawlers attack the Sworn caravan headed for the capital, and only Red and Vixor survive, the two must rely on each other to make it out of the perilous wilderness alive.

PROLOGUE

THE ALPHA'S ELITE werewolf fighters, the Sworn, came for my father on the night of my tenth birthday. As long as I live, I'll never forget that night. Every detail is branded upon my mind with excruciating clarity.

The evening began dreamily. My stomach had been twisting in anticipation of presents and dessert all day. My mother had baked a cake and drizzled it with honey. A ring of honeysuckles plucked fresh from the edge of the forest surrounded the cake, and I spent all of dinner staring at it. My grandmother was there, her hair still dark brown with only a few silver streaks in it at the time, her eyes the same unclouded gray, but they were merry when she looked at me. She smiled more then, even though the world was full of danger and uncertainty, even though our country had been ruled by werewolf overlords since she was a little girl, and their magic had tainted everything, even our forests and the animals that lived in them.

My best friend and neighbor, who lived in a brown house accessible via a path through the tangled woods that surrounded our home, a dark-haired boy named Kassian, was there to celebrate with us. I remember how he stole a honeysuckle blossom from the bunch around the cake and passed it to me under the table, our fingers brushing against each other. I broke off the stem of the flower and pressed the hole that was left to my tongue when my parents weren't looking. I'll never forget how Kassian smiled at me when the bubble of summery sweetness spread across my tongue. His eyes crinkled and a dimple appeared in his left cheek. He knew honeysuckles were my favorite.

After our dinner of beef stew and cabbage, my mother lit the candles and dimmed the lights. They sang to me while I held one hand over my mouth to hide my delighted smile. I was getting too old to be so giddy over things like birthdays. But something about the candles, the cake, the singing, the smiling faces—all of it washed away the tension and strain on my parents' faces. Even my grandmother looked happy for a moment in the light of those candles.

And Kassian. Kassian, my best friend since we were babies. In the last few weeks, I'd discovered that the way the sunlight fell across his hair made my hands sweat and my chest feel tight. I found myself daydreaming about touching his face, about holding his hand. And when I blew out the flames, I wished Kassian and I would be friends forever, whatever else happened between us.

The gifts came after the singing. My mother gave me a box wrapped in a flour bag. I opened it and found a honeysuckle-embroidered collar for my dresses that she'd knitted from her precious stash of yarns. After that came a doll, even though I was growing too old for them, its button eyes blue and its hair the same color as Kassian's. My grandmother reached into her pocket and produced a wooden ring polished to butter smoothness, unwrapped and still warm from its place next to her hip. My father's eyebrows lifted at it, and a wordless glance passed between them, but I didn't understand the significance of their silent communication.

"It's nothing," my grandmother said then, in response, and my father grunted.

Then, my father's gift. The box was heavy, and I set it in my lap, my whole body tightening with anticipation as I lifted the lid and dipped my fingers beneath the paper laid on top of the contents inside.

Something dense and soft met my hand. Fabric, black threaded with gold filigree that winked and flashed in the dim light of our kerosene lantern.

I lifted the gift from the box, and velvety folds spilled over my knees and across the floor.

A cloak.

One side black and gold, the other side a deep, vibrant red.

My grandmother drew in a sharp breath, as if someone had slipped a knife between her ribs.

"Dan," she said to my father. "What are you doing?"

"It's hers," he replied, his voice flat and firm at the same time, the tone he used when he was feeling unyielding. "It's always been hers."

"Don't be a fool," she replied angrily.

I only dimly heard them, for I was captivated by the cloak. I spread my palm against the silky feel of it, tracing the embroidered flowers, turning the edge of it this way and that to admire the way the light bounced across the threads. Something about it seemed to call to me deep in my bones. There was power in this cloak. Magic. Tendrils of it teased my fingertips as I ran them across the fabric lightly. Touching it felt like an echo of when I'd brushed against the electric fence that ran around the fields where Farmer Eliazar, the only one in the village with a windmill that produced power, kept his cattle.

The sensation faded, leaving only fabric, but I knew what I'd felt.

My grandmother reached across the table and put her hands on the cloak as if to take it from me. A noise of protest tore from my throat. My father grabbed her wrists.

"Don't," my grandmother said again to my father. This time, it sounded like an order.

I lifted my head, and my stomach curled at my grandmother's expression. I glanced from my father's face to my grandmother's in confusion. They were both grim.

My mother stood silently and busied herself with the dishes, leaving them to glare at each other. Kassian sat quietly, looking as confused as I felt.

"You can't stop it," my father said tightly.

My grandmother's face went as rigid as a statue's. "I can stop it," she hissed to my father. "I'll do everything in my power to stop it. I won't lose her, Dan. Not Meredith."

I was frightened. What did my grandmother mean, lose me? How was giving me a cloak going to cause me to be lost?

"Daddy?" I asked, the word scraping in the sudden silence.

"Later," my grandmother said. "We'll discuss this later."

"There's nothing to discuss," my father said. He scooped up the cloak and put it back in the box. He closed the lid and put it beneath my bed that sat in the corner. "Who wants some cake?" he asked, forcing joviality into his tone.

My grandmother's jaw tightened, but she allowed him to brush the matter aside for now. The tension eased in the room, and the lantern seemed to brighten. My mother returned to the table and straightened her hair with one hand. I remember how her fingers trembled against her forehead. She mustered a smile for me and asked, "How about an extra big piece, Red?"

"Don't call her Red," my grandmother said before I could speak. "Her name is Meredith. It's a beautiful name."

It was an old, stupid argument. My grandmother must have still been feeling surly to invoke it. I was a girl of many names. My family called me Red because of my hair, which had been red as a radish when I was born, and the fact that the word was nestled between the other letters of my given name, Meredith. It was a short, no-nonsense kind of moniker, and I never thought it was that pretty. It tasted like a lump on my tongue. Red. Short, easily shaped into a shout, a curt command, a snap. Friends called me Mere, and I was used to hearing that yelled by other children as they waited for me at the gate so we could venture into the edge of the forest to pick blackberries and search for fresh eggs. Only my grandmother and my teachers ever called me Meredith, which was prettier, but unfamiliar to my ears. The word was undulating, lispy, fancy. I used to practice whispering it to myself as I stared into the mirror, searching for myself in the sound of it. But I never seemed to find my identity in that name.

Kassian, my Kassian, called me Erie, and I liked that name best of all. It made me think of wind-swept skies and rippling cloaks and soaring high above the forest, higher than any Sworn or treecrawler could reach. It made me feel safe, but also somehow adventurous.

"She's our daughter. We'll call her whatever we want," my father said to my grandmother.

"She's my granddaughter," my grandmother replied icily. "Her hair isn't even red anymore. It's brown. It doesn't make sense, and besides, she has a perfectly good name."

My mother remained silent. She wasn't afraid to argue with my grandmother, but she picked her battles. Tonight, she seemed determined to let my father do the fighting.

"Lots of people call me Mere, Grandmother," I interjected. "And the butcher's son calls me Merry."

"The butcher's son has a Chosen for a sister," my grandmother spat. "Do you really want the brother of a Chosen calling you anything?"

"Those poor girls," my mother murmured in my grandmother's direction. "It isn't their fault, Delphine."

"Let's eat some cake," my father declared, because this was another fight brewing.

"Yes, please," I said about the cake. I was feeling scared because of the way the adults were acting, and the end of the words squeaked when they left my lips. I didn't want to think about the Chosen—girls who were dragged from their homes and

239

marked with claw-drawn tattoos by the Sworn, marks made to designate them as future breeders for the werewolf army. I wanted to pretend everything was happy this evening. I wanted to pretend that there was no Alpha ruling us as a dictator, that there were no dangers prowling the forest that grew thick and wild around our village and farm, and that there were no disagreements between the people I loved about the right way to think about these things.

Kassian grabbed my hand beneath the table, and I felt a thrill of excitement despite everything else. I ate my extra big piece of honey carrot cake and held Kassian's hand, and for ten minutes, even though my grandmother and my parents had argued and my grandmother still looked quietly furious, I felt safe and whole.

After dinner, my father asked me to take the scraps to the compost heap. "You're old enough to go alone," he said, with a pointed look in my grandmother's direction when she tried to protest. "Take your new cloak."

The night air smelled sweet as I stepped onto the back stoop. The forest lay black with shadows, the branches of the trees moving faintly in the wind. Our house huddled right up against the woods. In the distance, I could see the feathery peaks of the vertical forest against the starry backdrop of the sky. The place that had once been a city with towers of silvery steel. Now, it was overgrown with so many vines and trees that it looked like the earth had reached leafy green fingers up to touch the sky.

One day, when I was old enough, my father had promised to take me there. To show me the secrets and wonders of the world before the Alpha and the Sworn.

I couldn't wait.

The cloak lay heavy and soft against my shoulders. I felt older wearing the weight of it, taller. Braver. Stronger, even. As if I could fight off any threat. I wore it with the scarlet side out, and I imagined that I stood out against the shadows like a drop of blood on coal, like a fighter for the resistance, as I strode into the backyard behind our cabin. I felt the faintest prickle of magic singe my skin again.

Crickets sang loudly, and the grass whispered around my ankles as I made my way to the compost heap, located a stone's throw away from the house so we wouldn't get raccoons rustling beneath our windows in the night while we slept.

I took my time in the yard, enjoying the feel of the length of cloak sweeping behind me like the train of a lady's gown. The weight of the cloak emboldened me. Usually, I scurried through my chores, nervous in the darkness with the forest at my fingertips, imagining invisible eyes were watching. But this time, I pretended I was a queen walking through her garden, regal and composed. The cloak dragged across the dew-soaked wildflowers. One day, it would fit me. It was a woman's cloak, made for a full-grown future self.

As I walked, the hem snagged on the thrusting roots of the Thorn Trees that rose from the soil like the grasping hands of buried zombies. We hacked them back, but they grew with a speed and stubbornness that rivaled every other plant in the forest, because they were magic. They'd burst into our world at the same time as the werewolves, spreading like fire across civilization along with the dreaded disease of the land that we called the Spore, a magic plant-disease that spread horrors in its wake.

I stopped to free myself from a Thorn Tree tendril, rubbing my thumb over the embroidery at the edges once more. A thrill lanced through me to think that this beautiful cloak was mine. I felt like a queen, and so I paused to lift my chin as if accepting the bows of my subjects before I raised the bucket to upend the contents over the compost heap.

I was dumping the scraps when the Alpha's elite werewolf soldiers came.

I had never seen the Sworn before, but I'd heard stories. Whispers of how they were fast as the wind, and just as silent. How they were taller and more muscular than the humans they looked like. The stories also said they had faces like monsters and eyes that glowed the cold blue of the moon on a frosty night, but the Sworn wore black wolf masks, so I didn't see their faces as they melted from the shadows of the forest in silence. They surrounded the house before I heard anything at all.

The first indication of trouble was a glass breaking.

And then my mother's scream.

I whirled, the cloak swirling around me. I saw the figures surrounding the cabin. They were as quick and lithe as ghosts. They wore the black armor of the Sworn—thorny arm shields and chest plates, and helmets fashioned from metal to look like wolves' heads.

They were like monsters from the deep forest.

Every person I loved was inside that cabin. Mother, Father, Kassian, Grandmother.

A gasp wrenched from my lips.

One of the Sworn turned its masked face toward me at the sound of my exhalation. The wicked wolf face glinted like a death mask in the pale moonlight. His curved shoulders, powerful beneath his armor and cloak, tensed.

I stood, feet rooted to the ground, a shout frozen on my tongue. My heart thundered. Surely the Sworn saw me. He would cross the grass and kill me with one swipe of his arm-shield. The thorny spines along it would slice my throat.

I wanted to run, but I couldn't move.

I couldn't breathe.

Like a fawn discovered by a predator, I was locked into place, trembling, my limbs like lead.

After an eternity, the Sworn turned back to the house and slipped inside. It was as if he hadn't seen me at all.

Another scream split the night, and I heard the sound of a struggle that ended in a dying gasp. The light in the house went out.

They emerged from the house, and I couldn't see how many of them there were. One wrenched his mask from his face, and moonlight caught his features. He looked just like a man.

I didn't understand. Where was his fur, his monstrous, doglike mouth?

The Sworn bled away into the shadows, rushing past me like wind, and I was alone.

Time seemed to swell and slow around me. My heartbeat felt as lethargic and final as the hand of a dying drummer in my chest. My thoughts sorted from their tangle and presented themselves one by one. Hide in the shadows. Run to the door and call for my mother. Stay here and never move again.

The house stood before me, corpse-like. I knew in my bones what I'd find if I went inside.

So, I didn't go inside. I stayed there, paralyzed, the cloak pooled around me, a cry stuck in my throat, and unshed tears blinding my eyes.

It felt like years had passed before a hand touched my shoulder. I jolted as time snapped back to its normal speed, my heart slamming in terror as I rose to fight.

But it was Grandmother.

She put a finger to her lips and helped me up. I was shaking, but her hands were strong and steady. I turned toward the cabin, my expression hopeful.

The windows were still dark.

Hope struggled up in my chest. My parents? Kassian? I turned back to my grandmother, looking into the forest behind her for them.

There weren't there.

My grandmother lowered her gaze and shook her head.

The second grief of losing them after that brief and wild hope struck like a slap. A hole opened inside me. Tears rolled down my cheeks, but I made no sound. I couldn't. It was as if my voice had been sucked from my throat.

My grandmother put something into my hand. I turned my palm over and looked down. My gifts— the ring she'd given me, and the collar-necklace my mother had made. More tears flooded my eyes.

She reached out and traced one finger down the cloak. I'd put it on with the red side out, but still, the Sworn had not seen me in the shadows.

"You were protected," my grandmother whispered as if reading my mind. "The red side of the cloak shields the wearer from the eyes of the Sworn. What

244

a happy incident of defiance on your father's part, and yours for wearing it. He was right to give it to you tonight. I wish I could tell him he was right." She fell silent again. She turned her head toward the house as if trying to make a decision.

"Can we go back now?" I ventured to ask.

"No, Meredith," my grandmother said gently. "There is nothing there that you want to see. Come. You're going home with me."

My grandmother reached out her hand, and I took it, and we stepped together into the forest.

NINE YEARS LATER

CHAPTER ONE

I WAS ON my way to a hanging.

The cloak that had saved my life as a ten-year-old child lay around my shoulders again, the black side facing out this time, the golden embroidered flowers shimmering faintly under the early morning sunshine. Dread lay in my belly like a dead snake, but determination danced atop it like cold fire.

The cart I drove rattled on the cobblestones of the city street as I steered it left toward the correctional yard and the gallows. My stomach curled into a hard ball as I caught sight of the structure and the rope that dangled from it. The noose, twisting in the wind. The hangman, leaning against the steps, smoking a cigarette with a bored expression on his face.

I pulled the cart to a stop and climbed out. My pulse hammered in my throat as I approached the steps.

When I reached the hangman, I licked my dry lips and tried to summon moisture into my throat. The wind blew, making the cloak flutter around my ankles. It was not quite autumn, and the air was still heavy and humid even in the early morning.

The hangman looked up, his eyes bright and brown as they met mine. Human eyes, instead of the strange moon-silver irises of the werewolves. He wasn't a Sworn. He was human.

A traitor to his kind.

He was young, with curly black hair and smooth brown skin. I'd imagined the hangman to be a monster, burly and cruel-faced, with a mask on and a crooked, sadistic smile. But this young man looked more tired than anything else. Tired and defeated, as if he'd already seen enough nightmares for a lifetime.

Still, I hated him.

I began, "I am here to formally protest the execution of—"

"Can't yet," he interrupted, cutting off my prepared speech. "You have to wait until they arrive." He took another drag of his cigarette and turned his head to blow the smoke away from us both.

"When are they arriving?" I asked. "The edict said sunrise."

For a split second, I was terrified that I'd been too late, that he was mistaken somehow or thinking of a different wagon of prisoners, but my fears were soothed at the man's reply.

"These things rarely happen on time," the hangman said. He finished his cigarette and dropped it to the stones, grinding out the burning bit with the heel of his boot. "Little warm for a cloak, isn't it?"

I drew the folds around me stiffly. "Executions chill my blood."

He jerked his chin to say he didn't care as he turned away. I stepped back to the side of the cart to wait.

If there was any mercy left in this world, I wouldn't be forced to wait too long.

I heard the procession before I saw them. The thud of the brute-beast's feet on the road, the creak of the execution cart's wheels. The gray-skinned behemoth swung into view, drawing the wooden vehicle with the cage in the back, two Sworn sitting in the driver's seat, wearing their black armor and masks, and three men huddled inside, dressed in rags, their hands curled around the bars between them and freedom.

My eyes found those of the one I sought.

Neil.

On his way to his execution, and still, he shot me a cocky smirk and an exaggerated salute in an effort to make me smile. Only the tension at the edges of his mouth and eyes and the stiffness of his shoulders betrayed his terror.

My heart pounded harder. I didn't smile back. My lips were too stiff to force into the shape of the lie.

He didn't know why I was here. He must think I'd come for moral support. To watch the escape.

He was expecting a rescue, of course.

But not from me.

The prison cart stopped, and the two Sworn stepped down to open the cage. They were tall and muscular. Their black, sculpted body armor seemed to suck all the light into its wicked depths, and their wolf helmets made them look even more inhuman. They moved with a sinuous grace that unsettled me, a kind of animal fluidity that left me prickling with unease like a mouse in the presence of a snake. While I'd gotten more glimpses of them since the day my family had been murdered, and I knew they looked human beneath the armor, I still thought of them the way the stories described them— monstrous, with faces like dogs beneath their masks, and hard bodies ridged with unexpected skeletal protrusions and masses of dark, wiry fur beneath their black armor.

The Sworn prodded the men onto the cobblestones. The prisoners' hands were tied together in front of them, the ropes trailing like leashes on the ground. Neil's face turned toward the gallows, and his smile slipped. His fingers, I noticed, were trembling.

The Sworn seized Neil by the arms and pushed him toward the wooden staircase up to the gallows. One, two, three steps up to the platform. His feet moved too fast.

My opportunity was passing by in microseconds.

I swallowed as he faced the executioner, still wearing that smirk across his mouth like a bandit's bandana. The morning wind stirred his hair, and he lifted his chin, confident, as the hangman read his crimes to the pitiful assembly—the Sworn, the other prisoners, and me. No one else had come in the misty dawn to witness this hanging. There were far too many hangings to attract much notice anymore.

The hangman's voice carried through the stillness. "I hereby charge you, Neil Grimmick—"

No, wait. I was wrong. Someone else had come. I spotted a carriage in the distance, half-hidden by the fog. A man stood beside it, his jewel-encrusted hand resting on the edge of the door to the carriage. His long, silvery hair was tied back from his face. He had a hawkish nose and full, pouting lips that sneered so perfectly we used to whisper among ourselves during his speeches that he must practice the look in front of his mirror to get it right.

Governor Creeb.

He'd come to watch Neil die.

The hangman was still speaking the sentence. "— Of seditious acts against the Alpha and his kingdom, and for transcribing treasonous words upon a government building."

Neil grinned. He was still waiting for his rescue.

250

The hangman placed the noose around Neil's neck.

This was my moment. Fear shot through my limbs like a jolt of electricity. I wet my lips and stepped forward, summoning every ounce of courage I possessed as I opened my mouth and prepared to bring every eye upon me.

"Wait," I called.

Neil's eyes fell upon me. In the distance, the governor's head swiveled in my direction.

The hangman looked bored. Tired. As if this were all some pointless charade.

"I am here to formally protest the execution of Neil Grimmick," I said, the words I'd memorized the night before stumbling off my tongue. "For reasons of illegitimacy."

"And what illegitimacy is that?" the hangman asked.

Neil gazed at me sharply, alert now. He had been expecting a rescue from his friends. Not this.

He didn't know that they weren't coming, that they'd been arrested too. There was no plan. His friends had not been able to make one. Two of them were still inebriated from the night before that had gotten him into this mess, and the others were cooling their heels in the jail across town. They'd been caught after him.

There was only me. Me and my ill-advised, harebrained plan to save him. It wasn't the flashy, heroic, resistance fighter-style of Neil's friends. I didn't have arrows or swords. I didn't have gas canisters.

But I did have something of value. A secret, one Neil didn't know.

"What—what are you doing, Red?" Neil said slowly. As if he were stringing his understanding together bead by bead.

"He didn't write those things," I said. I forced the words out, knowing I could not go back once I had spoken them. Dread dropped like stones into my lungs. I couldn't breathe.

"No?" the hangman asked.

"No," I said. "Because I wrote them, and I'm here to surrender in his place."

There was a heavy, silent moment.

"Red?" Neil called, his voice breaking with alarm. "Red! No! This isn't the plan!"

I refused to look at him, lest I lose my resolve.

In the distance, I saw Governor Creeb frowning as he watched.

Creeb was not fond of changes to the plan. But of course, he wanted the perpetrator punished. He was a stickler like that. He gave a nod to the hangman.

The Sworn came forward and took me by the arms, one on each side as if I were a threat, a dangerous criminal who needed to be restrained. Their gloved hands were strong, their fingers crushing my upper arms in powerful grips that elicited a gasp from my mouth before I could stifle it.

The hangman unceremoniously lifted the noose off Neil's neck and shoved him aside.

"You're free to go," the hangman said. "Get off the platform."

"I don't understand," Neil said, desperate now. "I was the one who was arrested."

"And she just confessed. We have our traitor. Now go."

The Sworn marched me toward the steps, past the other prisoners with their mouths hanging open, their expressions a mixture of surprise and pity at what was about to happen to me.

I took the final steps alone and stopped before the dangling noose. The hangman looked me over with a little more respect now. And pity.

"Sorry, girlie," he said as he lifted the rope.

The rope settled around my neck. I closed my eyes—a flutter—and took a deep breath. They hadn't bound my hands yet, so the hangman stepped around to my front to do it. He turned over my right wrist and swore under his breath. His face turned white as ash, and he stepped back as if he were afraid to touch me.

"Why aren't you wearing your colors? Why didn't you say what you are?" he hissed. "I didn't know! I could have killed you!"

The Sworn at the steps lifted their heads at his words. Their blank, covered faces glittered in the sun, and my stomach curled into a knot.

On my wrist, a raised red mark of two circles overlapping lay like a hideous birthmark. Like the body of a dead snake. Like a brand. A hateful, ugly, jarring scar of a tattoo.

You see, I had a secret. One I'd hidden for years from everyone, including my friends, even my beloved Neil. Only my grandmother had known the truth. Only she had seen the mark I always kept carefully hidden.

Only she had known I was one of the Chosen.